I0730714

Library of Congress Cataloging-in-Publication Data.
Comicker Press
Strawberries & Stones / Ingrid Wolfe

ISBN: 9978-0-9974873-7-4
Library of Congress Control Number: 2024946096

www.ComickerPress.com

~ Created and Written by ~
Ingrid Wolfe

~ Cover and Illustrations by ~
Jake Pleshe

Deep in the Dreaming Grove,

the mist was getting heavier, rolling in across the streets of the Argentum Bastion. It was a time when most would go inside and settle in for the night, besides the night patrols. The faeries would be out soon, and more of the ones best avoided with such low visibility. Arleith, though, paced at the town border, deep in thought. The deep purple hue under his silver scales made him blend naturally into the darkness. Most people would have stopped to encourage him to get indoors, but if they weren't looking for him, they didn't notice him. The dragonborn was normally a very calm and collected person, but with the amount of visitors from the other clans in the last few weeks, he was starting to worry. A few walked past him, though no one said anything, despite the double glances he noticed through the fog.

He didn't really care and ignored them as his clawed feet dug into the mossy forest floor. All the clans had been showing up. The gold clans, the bronze and the brass clans, even the copper clans had all arrived within a few days of each other and Arleith was one of the few to notice that not all of them had left yet. It was fairly easy to figure out that there was only one thing being discussed by their leaders and the leaders of the Sivak Clan. Especially with the reduced patrols and increased drills for all active and reserve members of the military. War. There was a distinct possibility of it, at least.

"What did you get yourself into, Frostbite?" Arleith muttered to himself as yet another envoy went into the Praetorian Council chambers.

It had been four months since Gol'rotta had left. She hadn't said a word to her family, her squad, or anyone for that matter. As her lieutenant, Arleith had come to expect snap decisions that were often considered impulsive by others. As someone who had deep feelings for her though, he was worried. There was a glimmer of hope when a centaur arrived with a message for the Praetora's eyes only. Most diplomats asked for the Praetor first, despite often being redirected to the Praetora. The commotion and not so subtle protests of the Praetor himself confirmed what Arleith suspected. Gol'rotta was alive, alive and had probably kicked open a hornet's nest of political problems. But that had been a month ago now, and there hadn't been more word beyond that.

"Lieutenant… lieutenant? Lieutenant! Hey, lieutenant!"

Arleith finally stopped his pacing and looked up. A smaller, female dragonborn was flagging him down and by the wheezing of her breath when she finished jogging up to him, she had been for a while.

"Hey, Cricket," Arleith said dryly. "How'd it go?"

Strawberries and Stones

Toy'wl, mostly referred to as Cricket, caught her breath after a few more puffs of air before standing upright. "They… they gave me a promotion! Starting tomorrow I'm going to be assigned a squad. I'm-I'm so sorry."

Arleith softened his expression, something that wasn't the easiest for him to do with all the extra spurs and spines that covered his body, besides the already impressive set of horns. "Don't worry about it. This is a big moment for you. Don't cheapen it by worrying about me."

"It's not fair," Cricket blurted. "Everyone knows you deserve it more than anyone."
"I'm a ranger, that's just how it is," Arleith shrugged. "Congratulations."
Cricket accepted his offered hand. "I've been asked to send you to see the Praetor and Praetora too. Separately. I honestly can't guess what they want to say."

"One way to find out, I guess. We'll grab a drink to celebrate later, okay?" Arleith clapped a hand on her shoulder and gave her a nod.

Cricket nodded, but he could see the concern etched on her face before he turned away. The best thing to do was to act like everything was fine, he decided. It wasn't like he could hide it from a squadmate, but there wasn't any reason to upset her. Making his way to the longhouse was easy enough, even without a good field of view. Arleith had memorized the streets long ago, and came to the firefly lit lanterns that illuminated the entrance. Without bothering to knock, he pushed his way through the door.

Within an instant, he had two crossbows aimed at him, a spear at his throat and the hulking figure of one the bigger clan members bearing a battleaxe blocking him off from the rest of the room. Arleith didn't flinch, eying them all before a deep and commanding voice put them at ease.

"I didn't expect you to arrive so quickly, lieutenant."

The four dragonborn guarding the room parted to show the largest member of the clan. Well, Arleith couldn't help but smirk to himself at the thought, biggest until Gol'rotta gets back. Praetor Kal'bortaash sat in his high backed oak chair, the trim and armrests carved with intricate designs of dragons and ice formations.

"Just my duty, sir," Arleith shrugged. "Not like I'm doing anything anyway."

Kal'bortaash's face went smug as he propped up his elbow and casually leaned against his fist. "I suppose you'd like to get a new assignment like your fellow

A Tale From the Argentum Bastian

lieutenant. Though I suppose she outranks you now, so that's not appropriate anymore."

Arleith had been baited many times by the Praetor. It had only worked once before. "That would be correct, sir."

"The Praetora believes that Captain Gol'rotta will return," Kal'bortaash continued. "Personally, I have my doubts. It's likely she's not even alive."

Arleith could feel his jaw tightening, but he remained cordial. "She'll be back."

"As you and my wife seem so sure, I'll have to leave you at your current station until she does return. If she does," Kal'bortaash said with a spreading grin. "I'm not sure what you see in her to be so blindly… loyal."

The emphasis and contempt behind an arrogant smile was taunting him, goading Arleith to say or do something about it. Something that made him admit what most of the clan knew but didn't say out of respect for Captain Gol'rotta and her lieutenant. Knowing that if he did open his mouth it would most likely be something that would get him in trouble, he remained silent. Rear fangs grinding together, he maintained eye contact with the leader of the clan until a softer, but no less commanding voice broke the silence.

"Lieutenant, if you are finished, please meet with me in my office," the Praetora, B'lanna cut in from a doorway .

Arleith glanced up before locking eyes with the Praetor again. "We done?"

Kal'bortaash looked annoyed at the interruption, but let Arleith go with a dismissive wave. "Consider yourself on active duty still, but without a captain you'll remain in reserves. That's all I had left to say."

Alreith saluted, standing at attention with his right fist over his heart, then ducked into the next room over. The Praetora's office was much different than any other place in the Argentum Bastian. It almost looked more like their archives with all the shelves of books, stacked full and overflowing even. Despite having to make stacks on tables and her desk of the dozens that didn't fit on the shelves, it was still neat and tidy inside. Praetora B'lanna was sitting at her desk again, going over parchments and arranging them as she finished. There was no argument, she was beautiful. Her face was narrower and her scales smoother than most of the clan, the light blue undertone of her silver scales making her look like ice on the ocean. Arleith was one of the few that hadn't shown interest in her while growing up. Another twinge of anxiety started in the back of his head as he thought about it. She and Gol'rotta, her cousin, were the same age.

B'lanna put what she was working on down and politely cleared her throat as she caught his attention drifting far from the room. "Is there somewhere else you need to be, lieutenant?"

Arleith shook his head clear again and turned to face her. "No, ma'am. Sorry, ma'am. You need me for something?"

B'lanna eyed him carefully for a moment before continuing. "I asked you here because of the rumors of increased Fey activity lately. Have you noticed anything suspicious or out of the ordinary?"

"Besides the fog tonight, no, not really," Arleith snorted. "Wouldn't your sister be the expert on that topic? Wouldn't hurt to talk to her."

His tone sounded less like a friendly suggestion and more like an accusation that B'lanna didn't miss. "Shut the door, please."

Arleith gave pause at that, but did as he was asked. As the door latched shut he saw B'lanna lean forward in her chair when he turned back around, propping her elbows on her desk and lacing her fingers together.

"Any particular reason you have an interest in my family relations?"

Arleith knew he was close to crossing the line already, but part of him was still itching for a way to vent his frustration. "I dunno, somebody has to."

Without even realizing it, he was holding his breath as he waited for her to respond. He wasn't sure what to expect, because he normally had a healthy amount of respect for her. Muscles tensing as she leaned her snout into her hands before straightening her back and looking him directly in the eyes, getting a read on him. It was like she was reading his mind like a book.

"You've been wound up for a fight since you walked in," her voice soft, concerned. "That's not like you."

Arleith relaxed and stared shamefully at the floor. The only person in the entire clan that might understand was Praetora B'lanna and she had never been anything less than pleasant towards him. "I'm worried about Gol'rotta. She's been gone… She didn't even… Sorry, I know you're not the right person to complain to."

A Tale From the Argentum Bastian

B'lanna glanced at the door for a moment. A quick, dark glance that held a level of contempt Arleith didn't think she was capable of. By his estimate, it was almost exactly where a specific high backed chair would have been in the next room over. "Considering the circumstances of her departure, I've convinced the Elders that we treat this as a leave of absence for her mental health. I'm running out of leniency though."

"Want me to go get her?" Arleith offered. "Absolutely not," B'lanna snapped immediately.
Her harsh response seemed to have surprised herself, but Arleith took it as an opportunity to use it as an opening for his own frustrations. "Keeping in mind I'm off duty when I say this, but why the hell not?"

B'lanna tried her best to regain her composure, but the subject had her visibly flustered. Her voice wavering slightly, she added with insistence, "I can't just have her dragged back here! I'm

fairly certain she resents me enough right now as it is! No, we leave her be and let her return on her own."

"That's absolute hag shit," Arleith spat.

"Lieutenant, you are the only one not of my blood I would allow to speak to me like that, but if you do not compose yourself, I will enforce proper military decorum," B'lanna glared at him. "Do not think that I haven't sat up every night wanting to go out and get her myself, position be damned."

He cleared his throat and avoided eye contact as he straightened his shoulders. "I'm sorry. Really. It's just- I don't like this. What happened? What did her letter say?"

"I can't get into those details," B'lanna shook her head. "But… it's not good."

"Everyone is suspecting war," Arleith said bluntly. "We haven't had all the clans here at once in nearly 150 years."

B'lanna gauged him carefully, eventually looking sidelong at a very worn piece of parchment and touching it with her fingertips. "It's… a very distinct possibility. And another reason you cannot go looking for her. We might be dealing with Frostbane."

Arleith felt his heart quicken at the same time his insides felt like they had been scooped out and left him hollow, blood running even colder with fear. "You're not seriously considering abandoning her for plausible deniability…"

B'lanna's eyes turned away from his, glossy and gathering frost in the corners, making her held back tears hard to hide from Arleith's keen eye. "It comes straight from the Council of Elders.
Until we know for sure we have all of our allies in agreement, we are not to make further contact with Captain Gol'rotta."

"You can't be serious," Arleith barely managed to choke out. "How can they overrule your authority?"

"There was sufficient evidence to suggest my judgment is clouded in this matter and so the council set this course with the approval of the Praetor. In the name of what's best for the clan," B'lanna said quietly. "Please understand, this does not leave this room. I tell you this because I thought you would be the only one who might understand."

Arleith did understand. Putting his own feelings about the politics aside, he knew exactly what B'lanna was feeling. There was no doubt she cared for her cousin. They were raised like sisters and were extremely close. To be put on the sideline when someone she cared about was in danger, to be unable to act due to rank and duty despite personal feelings, to be utterly helpless for the most important person in her life, to be unable to even talk to anyone about it. Arleith

understood perfectly. He moved closer to her, B'lanna's eyes squeezed shut as she tried to maintain her composure. There was a movement from the shadows as he got within reach. One of her Praetorian Guards had been there the whole time, unseen by the experienced ranger. He nocked an arrow, but did not draw it. A simple motion to show he was there and ready if he tried anything funny. A large drake next to him sat up and eyed Arleith, but seemed to be waiting for a command from her master before striking. Oddly though, they allowed him to pull her in for an embrace.

B'lanna hugged him tightly. "You know, you're absolutely right. This is hag shit."

Arleith chuckled dryly, releasing her and getting some assistance from the Praetora as a few of his spines and spurs snagged on her dress. "She'll be back. Probably without even needing backup. Hell, she's probably going to take on the Head Bitch herself if I know Gol'rotta."

"That's what I'm worried about," B'lanna said as she dabbed her eyes dry and gathered herself back together.

A Tale From the Argentum Bastian

"Yeah," Arleith said under his breath, "me too."

The Praetora dismissed him, returning to her paperwork as he stepped outside the large oak door. Kal'bortaash was still there, eying him with curiosity as the ranger strode out of the longhouse. Arleith ignored the glance and excused himself without a word. His mind matched the world around him, hazy and easy to get lost in. Rather than clear his head, Arleith decided it was time to exacerbate the problem and headed to the pub. There were several in the Argentum Bastion, but the one with the strongest drinks around was The Tipsy Pixie. Unlike the practical designs of all the other structures in the city, this was an establishment that was adorned with creeping vines that always seemed to be in bloom. The beams and logs that made up the structure were twisted and gnarled, as if warped by the wild magics around the area to make it look natural. It was suspected that the Seelie faeries around them were honored by the inclusion and put their favor on the building. The sign out front was that of a pixie with butterfly wings sitting on a toadstool, a wide grin and a playful wink on her face, hefting a tankard while leaning back far enough to look like she would fall back.

Arleith admired the sign for a bit. The auburn haired pixie always felt so familiar and oddly comforting, despite the gold-green bubbles over head indicating her inebriation. Something about it had always felt more real, as though it was a likeness of a real fairy and not just a mascot. There wasn't much comfort tonight, and he ducked his head in, keeping his vision low as he sat on a barstool. It was livelier than usual, which was saying something. There was a lot of music that somehow managed to still be heard over the roars and cheers from one of the off duty platoons. They were around a table, singing and chanting as the smallest adult member of the clan danced a jig on top of it. Barely visible above them, being a full foot shorter than the average dragonborn, there was no mistaking the young female with the pinkish undertones in her silver scales, making her shimmer like a rose pearl. Sivak Sutra'ber, or Pip as she was known almost exclusively by, was surprisingly the center of attention, pouring a mead into her

mouth without skipping a beat in her dance. Most of it washed over her head, but Arleith knew her well enough to know that it was most likely intentional. He had always kept close tabs on her as part of Gol'rotta's family.

"Looks like you're having a rough night, lieutenant," the bartender said. "Usual Frost Brandy for you, or something stronger?"

"Firebrand Whiskey," Arleith said. "No ice."

The bartender nodded with a look of understanding at the unusual request. As the name suggested, Firebrand Whiskey burned all the way down. It was particularly potent for the ice breathing Sivak, so such a request usually meant that someone wanted to get drunk and fast. "That kind of night?"

"And several hundred like it," Arleith muttered.

He tossed a few coins on the counter before the drink even arrived, grabbing the bottle rather than the glass when it was placed in front of him. Removing the cork with his teeth, the ranger guzzled the dark liquid down. He'd had it enough to not cough and sputter his frost breath around like most of the other Sivak would have, but it still made him clear his throat with a noise that sounded more like a rasping wheeze. He tossed a few more coins on the counter and slid the bottle forward, indicating he wanted another. Leaning his brow against his thumb and forefinger, he stared intently at the carved mahogany of the bar while blocking out the rest of the establishment from view.

There was little point in denying it to anyone anymore. He cared for Gol'rotta more than he cared about any other member of the clan. He had for years, but had never once been allowed to show it. First as her instructor for forest training, then as her lieutenant when she graduated from the military academy, forced to bury his feelings while serving in her unit. Arleith had tried so many times to get a transfer so that there wasn't a conflict of interest. They'd both even played around the idea when off duty, so he was fairly confident the feelings were mutual. But the Praetor, Kal'bortaash, had made sure they were always in the same platoon, always leader to officer. Now, there was a chance that the clan might abandon her to her death and still he was unable to do anything about it.

A second bottle was placed in front of him and again he yanked out the cork with his teeth. "Damn it all to hell."

He loved her. There was no other way to put it and he was tired of being put on the sideline by anyone other than Gol'rotta herself. It wasn't hard to figure out Kal'bortaash kept them in the same unit to torment her. He wasn't even sure how the rest of the clan could have figured out their feelings for each other since he knew something like that would happen. Taking a swig of the second bottle, he stood. Exile seemed pretty good at this point, so he might as well break some rules. He eyed Pip as she twirled on the table in the corner, a few of her platoon still around and egging her on. Arleith politely pushed his way through and got up in front, waiting for her to look down and notice.

Whether she was drunk or completely dizzy, it was hard to tell, but it took her a while to finally gain some focus enough to recognize him.

A Tale From the Argentum Bastian

"Spire!" she gasped with a drunken laugh. "Did you come to dance with me?" "I need to talk to you," he shouted over the din.
"Troops! My duty calls me elsewhere! I must away!" Pip saluted.

Arleith's eyes widened as she began tilting forward. She was going to drop face first onto the pub floor. While most clan members would have moved to catch her, the tiny dragonborn came with enough stigma that even though she had been partying with her unit, they all moved away, trying to not be the ones to touch her. Arleith shoved one person away so that he could get in and have her land on one shoulder. She went limp and hung there as his arm went around her waist to steady her. He hefted her to adjust the small drunk and walked out of the pub with her draped like a sack of potatoes on his shoulder.

Unsure if she was conscious as she ended up facing behind him, he called back to Pip, "What were you thinking?"

"That you wouldn't lemme fall," she giggled, "and I was right!" Arleith shrugged his free shoulder. "It was tempting though."
"But you still didn't," Pip was practically cackling. "Where are we going?"

"You're going to sober up and then there's something I want to ask you," he sighed.

Pip was almost immediately less limp, turning her body to try and face him while still being carried. "I'm sober now. We can talk."

Arleith decided to put her down gently and watched her stagger to her feet. He rolled his eyes and took another swig of the bottle of whiskey he'd taken with him. "I didn't feel like waiting around anyway. I wanted to ask for your help with something. It'll break a lot of clan rules though."

"You have me intrigued, Lefty. What could it possibly be?" She smirked to herself as she realized she made a rhyme.

"It's Gol'rotta, I-"

"I'm in," Pip cut him off.

"You don't even know what it is," Arleith looked at her incredulously.

Strawberries and Stones

"Okay, okay, jeez, I already said I'd do it. No need to twist my arm!" "Pip, this is serious," Arleith grumbled.
"It's for my sister. I don't care what the details are, I'm in," Pip said firmly.

It was rare to see such a determined and adamant look in the eyes of Sivak Sutra'ber. Arleith could recall maybe twice her entire life before this moment that she had it. Her stance was off kilter and she was swaying a bit, but her amethyst colored eyes were resolute where her body was not. Deciding he was a little too sober still to be just as sure, he took another few gulps from the bottle. He'd never defied the clan before and his own discipline was making it difficult to do so, despite his circumstances.

"You know how we're supposed to leave the gateway to the Feywild alone?" he rasped after a long draught. "I want to find it and I want to go through it. Thought you might enjoy tagging along."

"Spire…" Pip's face was laden with concern for the briefest moment before it cracked into a mischievous grin. "I love it even more! I'm so glad you told me the details now!"

Arleith couldn't help but chuckle. "First thing in the morning then?"

Pip brought a flat hand up to her brow over one eye, a human salute if Arleith remembered correctly. "You can bet on it! We could go now though."

Arleith smiled but shook his head. He hefted the nearly empty bottle for emphasis and said, "I'm going to need to sleep this off. Maybe it'll give me enough time to come to my senses."

"Gods, I hope not," Pip looked aghast.

"I wouldn't bet on it," he drained the last of the whiskey and tossed it with pinpoint accuracy into a bussing bin balanced on an open window ledge of the pub. "See you in the morning, Pip."

Despite the liquor in his system, sleep did not come easily to Arleith. Most of the night was spent staring at the ceiling, contemplating what would come next. He'd set himself up with a limited chance now that Pip was involved. Whether she acknowledged it or not, she was the expert on faeries in the clan. Any trist into their realm would need someone who knew how to deal with them and Pip was the best choice. No one really knew what she was up to in her free time, but it wasn't hard to see that the Dreaming Grove favored her immensely.

A Tale From the Argentum Bastian

Several questions ran through Arleith's mind. The first was if Pip would be enough. Her skills and manic charm weren't what he was worried about. It was the fact that they shared the forest

with the faeries, but venturing into their world could be seen as trespassing. Then there was the question of if they'd even be able to find it. If they did, would they be able to get back out? What would happen if they were caught by the clan? What kind of punishment would they get? All of these and more boiled down into one central and all encompassing question.

Was it worth it?

The answer was always, 'Yes'. At least for himself. Arleith did have some reservations about putting Pip, one of the two living blood relatives of the dragoness he loved, in danger for his own desires. It was probably the only thing he could have thought more thoroughly through had he been sober. That damage had already been done, which he was harshly reminded of when there was an unending, rapid knock on his door. Head pounding and unrested, he got up and opened the door. Pip was there, still knocking despite the new angle.

"How in the Nine Hells are you this energetic and not hungover?" he grumbled, gently grabbing her wrist to move her hand away from the door.

"I don't get hangovers," she beamed. "C'mon! It's morning! Time to get ready!"
"Yeah, yeah, come on in," Arleith sighed, moving aside so that she could enter. Darting in, she started going about making tea, starting with lighting the wood burning stove, while arguing with an unseen entity apparently directly on her shoulder. Arleith paid little mind to the conversation as he went about setting out his armor and weapons. Putting on a shirt, he began fastening the leather armor on himself. The Sivak didn't have a specific uniform for their soldiers. They were all allowed to pick fittings that suited their fighting style for comfort and efficiency. Like most of Arleith's clothing, his armor didn't have completed sleeves, because of his extra spines. Instead, he had leather wraps and separate pieces to cover what he needed to.

On the table were several belts and holsters for dozens of implements. Bandoleros of daggers, concealed wrist compartmented bracers for long darts, javelins, tomahawks, all small weapons for a dragonborn. All easily thrown. He began the ritual of checking the sharpness of all of them, making sure hilts and hafts were secured and strong. It was normally a task that might take someone a while, but for Arleith, he was well practiced in it.

Strawberries and Stones

Pip placed a mug with steaming tea, a fragrance of mint wafting up from it. "Here you go, that should help."

"Thanks," he nodded as he picked it up and sipped it. Pip scowled at him. "Don't say that."
"Just showing my appreciation," Arleith gave her a sidelong look.

"Then just say it like that," she huffed, but switched in an instant to childish curiosity. "Those don't match. Your set is wrong."

Arleith looked where she was pointing. One of the belts with multiple sheathed daggers had one odd one that was slightly longer and sporting a different design at the pommel. "Yup, it is."

Pip seemed to notice that he wanted the conversation to end there and dropped it for the time being. Like a kreshling wandering a new place, she stopped to touch and pick up everything in Arleith's home, asking questions about all of them. He didn't have a lot, so it didn't take long for her to get bored of that and start humming to herself and bounce off all of the furniture. She eventually settled on hanging upside down on his bed and whispering to her invisible friend.

Arleith didn't mind. It was almost endearing, really. He liked to imagine that's what a lot of the faeries were like. Happy and carefree in their day to day life. If anything she was usually more mature than she was acting at this moment, on a normal basis. As Arleith finished buckling the last belt he intended to take with him, he tilted his head to a ninety degree angle to be a little more upright to Pip.

"You okay today?" he asked. "You seem nervous."

"Pffft! No!" Pip laughed as she tumbled to the floor and sprang upright in a fluid motion. "Excited! What are we going to do there? Are there going to be snacks?"

"Nah, it'll probably be boring," Arleith shrugged. "We're just going to look for rocks."

"Rocks? ROCKS?!" Pip was borderline disgusted at the thought until something clicked in her head. "Oh! Rooooooooooocks."

She nodded slowly at him with a cheshire grin and a gleam in her eyes. Arleith snorted a short laugh and playfully shoved her. "What are you looking at?"

"You were trying to make me bored so I wouldn't come anymore," Pip eyed him in

A Tale From the Argentum Bastian

admiration. "But you didn't lie to me. Well played, my friend. I'm just too clever for you though."

Arleith shrugged. "Anything happens to you, your sister and your cousin will both kill me. And not at the same time."

"Ha! Well you already asked me and I already said I'd come! No take backs! You'll just have to make sure I don't die," Pip shouted triumphantly and stuck out her tongue.

Arleith was used to such antics, but he was never fully prepared for them. With no retort, he motioned with his head for them to head out. They stopped at the market, purchasing ample amounts of cream and honey to offer as gifts and appreciation to any faeries they might

encounter. Pip did lose interest as Arleith divided their purchase into proper offering amounts and decided to go back outside and make flower crowns and bracelets. Arleith was impressed enough to tuck them in his haversack as for more potential gifts, when Pip left them laying on the ground.

Provisions for themselves were also important. Several factors around the Feywild and even faeries themselves was that it was never a good idea to eat fairy food. There was no telling what it might do to someone and no telling how long the effects would last either. By extension, it was even worse to eat food offered by a fairy because of the pranks they liked to pull. People had fallen asleep for years, some had lost their minds, and other such types of stories that were common to hear. Another drawback was with the many shapes and sizes Fey creatures came in, it was impossible to tell if you were killing and eating a sentient creature or not since they could be anything from talking animals, to living plants, to the creatures people normally envisioned the Fey to be. About as stocked as they felt they could be to avoid such problems, they waited for nightfall.

When the mist started rolling in again, the two of them swiftly and silently slipped past their borders and into the grove. It was odd, at first. Watching Pip move with steadfast intent was hard to picture, and witnessing it, Arleith wasn't sure he cared for it. Her entire family stood out for one reason or another and to see her like this just felt so… plain. He knew the only reason she was being serious was because it was for Gol'rotta, but she had never honed her focus, preferring to dance around topics and pretend she didn't care. It made him nervous, seeing her act unlike herself. Only when they were far from the Argentum Bastion did Pip finally break her silence.

Strawberries and Stones

"I just realized that this is the longest I've gone without someone asking me about what happened to me when we hang out," she mused almost thoughtfully. "No wait! Now it is! Oh, but now it's been even longer! Wait, wait, now it's been the longest amount of time-"

"Suffice to say, every moment from here forward will be the longest," Arleith cut her off with a chuckle. "Or are you trying to imply you want me to ask?"

"Well most people only want to talk to me if they're going to ask about when I was little," Pip pouted. "Do you not like talking to me, Spire?"

"We talk just fine, Pip," Arleith said coolly.

"Yeah, but are you just forcing yourself to because you don't want to ask?" she pressed, but her eyes were wide with terror, like she was afraid of the answer.

"You disappeared for two weeks when you were four years old. You felt like it was only a couple hours. You followed a will-o-wisp, played with some faeries, and then everyone came running," Arleith recited. "I believe you. I believe that's how it happened for you. I figured you were sick of people asking questions you've already answered."

"I am!" Pip gasped a sigh of relief. "But, you know, I guess I thought it meant you didn't care."

"Well, I do care," Arleith assured her with a smile. "I'm not going to pry into your life, but if you ever feel like talking, I'll be there."

Pip gave one of her more sincere smiles and nodded. "That's a dangerous offer." "I'll take my chances."

They went back to trekking quietly, but the tension in the air Arleith had felt was much more relaxed. Pip hummed softly to herself and eventually started skipping through the underbrush of the forest. As the mist started shifting from the normal grey to a somewhat pinkish hue, they stopped and regrouped. Knowing they were getting close to the entrance to the Feywild, the two of them went completely silent and started combing the area. It could have still been miles away, or they already may have passed it. It was always hard to tell with faeries, so it never hurt to be doubly sure. By the time neither of them could save face and keep looking, they still hadn't found the gateway to the fairy realm.

They searched for days, always unsure if they'd already been to an area. There was always the chance that they had been tricked into trudging around in the same circle under some little prank a pixie might have enjoyed playing on them. Pip was fairly certain they weren't and Arleith was inclined to trust her judgment. It had been the reason he had asked her along. Maybe not the wisest choice in any other situation, but the best one for what they were doing. A week later and the two of them still hadn't found anything, but the plants were getting more wild and lush, so they knew they had to be on the right track.

"I'm tired of holding it in!" Pip fumed as she plopped down in their newest campsite. "I have to ask!"

Arleith knew what came next could be a serious question, but it could also be something like what his favorite color was. "What's up?"

"Which one of these spines is the one that grew so that you'd finally ask Frostbite out?" she flicked one of the spikey growths on his head. "That's what we're here for, right? You want to find a Tlhogh Stone."

Arleith shifted uncomfortably, avoiding eye contact. "Just going right for it there, aren't you?"

"Spire, Spire, Spire," Pip tutted and shook her head. "Everyone knows. Believe it or not, you're not great at hiding how you feel. You don't say anything, but it's all in your expression. Frostbite isn't much better either."

Arleith looked at her incredulously, but speechless all the same.

"Right now you're thinking 'There's no way I'm that obvious'. But you are," she finished in a sing-song voice.

"Alright," he conceded. "Yes, I want to give her a Tlhogh Stone. I thought I'd make it out of a gem no one else has. Something special…"

As he trailed off and went quiet, Pip smiled and eyed something just above her shoulder. "See? I told you! Now will you tell me where to find it?… Why don't you want him to come?… You trust me, right? Well I trust him… Yes it is different… You will?!… You're the best!"

"Sorry, I must have missed something," Arleith said cautiously.

Pip hissed through her teeth, first at Arleith, then at her shoulder. "Spire, stop saying that!… You can't change your mind!… Well the clan teaches us that it's polite to use that word…

Strawberries and Stones

Well how can he know he's offending you if you haven't properly introduced yourself?"

Arleith's eyes widened and he went into a deep and overly theatrical bow. "I beg your pardon. I regret that I was unaware I was in the presence of one of the fair folk."

"There, you see?" Pip beamed. "Spire, this is Clover."

Arleith looked at what appeared to be empty space where she was pointing, but bowed again. "It's a pleasure to meet you."

"You can see her?!"

"No," he admitted, "but I do believe she's there."

"She's going to show us the way!" Pip exclaimed. "Follow me!"

Arleith stuttered a moment, looking at the gear they'd just laid out. Pip didn't seem to notice or care, because she darted through the forest in hot pursuit of her unseen friend. He cursed under his breath and abandoned it, not wanting her to get out of sight. A brief panic went down his spine when he saw how far ahead she was. Pip was fast and the forest seemed to part for her, giving her a clear path where Arleith had to use his ranger training to maneuver his way through the dense forest. They sprinted the entire way, Arleith losing line of sight to Pip every once in a while and causing him to fall even further behind. Determined not to lose her altogether, he muttered a quick incantation and made a slight gesture with his hand. Before he had even finished he could feel a surge of power in his legs. With the energy coursing through him, he picked up his pace, gradually closing the distance between them until she suddenly stopped.

Skidding to a halt barely before knocking into her, he was about to ask if there was anything wrong until his eyes followed her gaze. Before them was a slight shimmer between two of the

larger trees in the area, a faint orange and purple sky in the distance. He glanced up and saw that the sky was still clear and blue above them. Leaning around, it was clear that what they saw was not around the trees before them. There would have been a view of the mountains if it was.

"Clover still here?" Arleith whispered, to which Pip nodded slowly. "You showing us the path is much appreciated, Miss Clover."

A Tale From the Argentum Bastian

Pip was fixated on the sight before her, jaw slack, but she did raise a thimble full of cream to her shoulder. When she let go, it hovered there a moment, the surface slightly disturbed. It began to rise without spilling a drop before it circled them and took off.

"Payment for the help?" Arleith asked, still quietly.

"No, I bet her I could lose you," Pip said as she stepped towards the gateway.

He chuckled and shook his head before going back to staring at the Fey Realm. "I always thought it was an actual gateway, but this… this is a Rift."

His smaller companion almost seemed like she was in a trance as her eyes shimmered with an expression he wasn't sure how to read. "I don't remember seeing this… but I feel like I knew that already…"

The Feywild was a dangerous place. Not necessarily just for the creatures that lived there and the games they played, but also how easy it was to get lost. To lose memories or to think you had only been gone a short time, only to find out years had passed, or even the opposite where someone might age and spend years looking for their way home, only to find out the world had basically stood still in their absence. Many of the Sivak Clan had fallen victim to such realities and based on Pip's experience, she had as well. The difference with her was that no one wanted to acknowledge it. Only adults that knew the dangers were taken seriously. But Pip, Pip was ignored. She had already been hatched small, and so she was kept separate from most other children. It shouldn't have been a surprise that she developed odd behavior for a dragonborn. But with her return it had gotten more pronounced. No one wanted to admit they had failed her as a child or acknowledge the possibility that the Fey had done something to her. And so she had always been an outcast in the clan, as far back as her memory could go. There had always been a chance that the Feywild might hold answers for her and her reaction to seeing the entrance proved to Arleith that she cared more than she let on.

He gently placed his hand on her shoulder, startling her back to reality. "Still want to go?"

"Of course," Pip smiled, again, more soft and genuine than usual. "You take a girl to the best places. Frostbite is going to be jealous."

There was a brief pause of hesitation from both of them before they walked together, side by side, through the Rift. There was a slight tingling sensation as they crossed the boundary, like pinpricks that weren't quite uncomfortable. A fragrance washed over them as they stepped onto the lush grass. The flowers around them closed as they adjusted their footing for the new environment. The aroma was sweet and the flowers slowly reopened as they were still taking in everything the view. The sky was still purple and orange, but now that they had the full view of the horizon, a reddish sun was high above them. It was strange and breathtaking, enough for them to take a few extra moments to appreciate all they were seeing.

Both at a loss for words, they gave each other a knowing look and pressed forward. Arleith was amazed at how many creatures he saw. While in the mortal realm, faeries preferred to stay invisible. It was rare to have a sighting even in the Dreaming Grove, but here they were everywhere. The lieutenant had never personally seen many of the fair folk, but now there were dozens within eyesight. With the comfort of their own realm around them, they didn't hide from the pair. As they passed through the meadow directly in front of the Rift, the vibrant flowers of colors that were almost impossibly bright would open up and sleeping faeries would stretch their wings and take to the sky. The variety between them was astounding. It seemed like every single one was unique in their own way, from their hair color to their wings.

It was a fascinating sight, but as they wandered, they noticed that the sky hardly ever changed. It grew brighter and dimmer on occasion, but there wasn't a true sense of night or day. A perpetual cycle of shifting dawn and dusk. It was hard to tell how long they'd been hiking, but Arleith could feel his eyes beginning to droop and his limbs getting heavy as the meadow started giving way to a thicket of twisted trees and vines.

"We better make camp. There's no telling how long we'll be walking if we wait for nightfall." Pip leaned against him and yawned. "Any idea where we're even headed?"
"Not really," Arleith admitted. "Nothing here seems to be working like it does at home. My best guess is to find a river."

She nodded. "I guess without a map we have no idea how close we might be. Shall we then?"

Arleith held his hands, indicating he didn't have any of their camping equipment. "I have a few rations in my satchel with the honey and cream offerings, but everything else got left behind."

Pip gasped in shock. "Why didn't you grab any of our stuff?" "Because you made a bet with a fairy," Arleith sighed.
"Oh yeah!"

A Tale From the Argentum Bastian

He rolled his eyes and took out a piece of the dried rabbit they had smoked the night before. They had used up everything they brought, but they were both skilled hunters and it had been easy enough to gather enough to eat. Here though, it was a different story. There were many tales of people that ate the wild flora of the Feywild, only to suffer one of several dozen ways. The fey were very protective of wildlife as well, so hunting was also pretty much out of the question.

Ripping the piece in half, Arleith sat next to Pip, handing her the larger portion. The two of them stared at the sky again, the purple having taken over most of what they could see, they assumed it was about the equivalent of night.

"It's weird looking up and not seeing stars ever," he said, taking a small bite.

"The faeries love them. That's why they come to visit so much," Pip smiled, holding her piece but seemed too interested in the view to eat. "Clover says that sometimes they pop up here, but it's only once in a blue moon."

"You must've known her a long time," Arleith glanced at her almost childlike face as she looked around.

"Ever since I could walk, she's been around," Pip's eyes were glistening. "She's always been there."

Arleith cleared his throat uncomfortably, wondering if perhaps she might resent the clan somewhere under her cheshire exterior. "So, any suggestions for tomorrow?"

"No," Pip stated absently. "But we should sing a song and leave some things out."
He grimaced at the thought. "You know I'm a terrible singer."
She faced him and smiled. "That's why you gotta. It doesn't matter how good you are, what matters is how much fun you have. Quit being stuffy, or you'll wake up with your dreads in knots."

Arleith put a hand to the back of his head where long, flexible scales grew in such a way that many other humanoid races considered it the equivalent of hair. The amount of dragonborn that had them was about the same as those that did not, but as with his spines and spikes, Arleith had more than usual and his were longer than most.

"I only know marching songs," he grumbled.

Pip just stared at him expectantly until he reluctantly sighed, awkwardly starting the first verse in a very flat and off key melody. To his relief, she joined him once she was satisfied with watching him squirm uncomfortably.

Strawberries and Stones

Arleith had heard her sing before. It was beautiful and soulful, invigorating the spirit or drawing tears from the most hardened soldier depending on what she sang. This time, she was obnoxiously going off beat and switching keys as if to spare him from embarrassment. In a way, it worked. He couldn't help but laugh, causing him to miss a few beats before getting back in tempo and singing louder. They went back and forth trying to drown each other out until they started gesturing and eventually standing and dancing as lights began to gather around them. They flickered and moved with their rhythm until Arleith went hoarse and had to quit. Grinning, he took a long drink from his waterskin as the lights all darted away when the singing ended.

"Told you!" Pip laughed as she collapsed onto the ground and stared at the sky. "You saw them, didn't you?"

"Yeah, I did," Arleith smiled and passed her the waterskin. "Were those all fairies?"

"Yup! They're really hard to make out for a while, but one day you'll see them all like I do," she beamed before pouring water into her mouth from a lying position.

His smile was having a hard time fading, despite how weary the two of them were. Placing his satchel on the ground to provide a semi-level surface in the grass, he placed out a small dish of cream and honey. Not being a mortal of many words, he didn't have much voice left after the musical duel, but with what he had left for the day, he managed to thank the faeries in a way they would appreciate before laying down.

"It was great having you at the party."

While he couldn't see any of them anymore, a gentle breeze touched his snout. Pip curled up into a tight ball nearby and continued humming to herself as they both drifted off to sleep.

It was impossible to tell what time of day it was when they woke up, or how long they'd actually been asleep. They both felt rested and full of energy though and were ready to continue onward. The two dishes were polished clean, which gained a smile from Arleith. As he put them away, he noticed a bracelet of flowers had been woven around his wrist. He chuckled to himself at the notation that he must have made a good impression, but it was still unnerving to think there was a creature out there who could do such a thing without him noticing. Pip was similarly garnished, though to a much greater extent with an entire weave of flowers and vines wrapped around her tail.

"I guess you won our little competition last night," Arleith nodded to draw her attention to her decoration.

"Of course I did. I had more fun than you," she said smugly.

Again with no retort, Arleith simply rolled his eyes with a subtle smile. They gathered what little they had and headed into the thicket. It was a beautiful forest, full of colors they had never seen

on the trees before. Some were similar enough to autumn leaves, but there were others that had deep blue coloration and others that were silver and gold in ways that looked like they were actually made of metal. The deeper they got though, the darker the entire area seemed to get. Trees that were grey and gnarled became more and more abundant, almost looking dead in the foreboding gloom that was surrounding them.

They remained quiet, but kept moving quickly. Not wanting to find their way into something they shouldn't, they changed course slightly when the earth began to shift to bog. They decided to stick to the very edge of it in hopes it would lead to a river. What felt like hours, that could have been days, passed until their persistence was rewarded. A river that drained into the bog they'd been skirting trickled peacefully in the eternal sunset. On the horizon there was a mountain in the distance that seemed to shimmer like the inside of a cracked geode.

"Shall we look?" Arleith asked.

"This is for Frostbite! If you want a stone that's the proper size for how amazing she is, we have to go up the river!" Pip admonished. "Maybe even to that mountain itself!"

Arleith threw his hands up in defeat. "Okay, okay, you're right. I'm just worried we're pushing our luck here. People are going to have noticed we're gone by now."

"So?" Pip asked, her expression serious again.

"So?" Arleith snapped back, but softened and nodded. "Yeah. So what?"

"That's right," Pip nodded. "If this is really love, then you've got to stop acting rationally. That's for after you're married."

Arleith snorted a small laugh and nodded. "Alright. Onward it is then."

Following the listing stream they eventually left the forest they had been in and entered a grassy plain. It was nearly three feet high, tinted slightly blue in the broad green leaves. A few clusters of trees dotted the landscape, but it was fairly open otherwise. Wading through the grass, Arleith was up to his waist and getting slightly tangled with his spines. Pip wasn't faring much better, up to her shoulders and barely able to see much around her. It was a little thinner and shorter near the riverbank, but the two preferred to walk even with each other instead of one being behind the other. Arleith decided to take the inland side, but it was still slow going.

They spotted a herd of centaur off in the distance, galloping together over the horizon. It took a while for them to fade away, but by the time they were completely out of sight, the grass was short enough to be manageable as it began shifting to what looked like a field of clovers. There were enormous bulb shaped flowers with their petals closed, but in full color, seemingly ready to bloom at any moment. As the sky began to shift darker, Pip excitedly, but quietly, pointed to movement in one of them. Arleith was busy examining them from a distance, noticing that the

base of the flower was level with the ground, lacking a stem when he was hit by a powerful and dizzying scent.

As the very tip of the bud opened, an explosion of pollen spilled into the air. Arleith didn't notice it in time and got a full breath that nearly knocked him to his knees. It was a strong aroma, not just floral, but sweet. Potent enough to make all of his other senses overloaded. His heart began pounding so hard it was as though someone was hammering on the inside of his ribs. With his vision swimming, he clutched his chest and reeled with his mind in a haze. Pip was saying something, her face covered by the cowl of her hood. Arleith couldn't hear her, he couldn't focus on her. Practically spinning, the only thing that seemed to be clear and steady was the opening pink flower petals. As they opened, the form of a nude woman with pale green skin, shimmering as if slightly damp and glistening in the odd light, was standing in the center. Her hair was the same pink as the petals of the flower around her, long pointed ears, far longer than any elf's, jutted back but were lost as she turned her head. She opened her eyes and there was nothing but black, shining like obsidian.

Dazed, Arleith lurched towards her. Pip tried grabbing his arm and pulling him back, but he barely felt her, easily shrugging off the much smaller dragonborn. Other flowers around them began opening and filling the air with even more pollen. None of them caught Arleith's attention enough as he walked toward this majestic, beautiful creature. Something was drawing him to her, as if she were the most alluring thing he'd ever set eyes on. In the back of his mind, some part of him screamed that there was something wrong, but he ignored it as she beckoned for him.

Pip wrapped her arms around Arleith's tail and dug her heels in, trying to at least slow him down, but it still wasn't working.

The creatures in the other flowers began to get irritated as Pip seemed to be resisting whatever was in the air. Arleith caught a glimpse of some other movement out of the corner of his eyes, but it wasn't important enough to him in the moment. All that mattered was this beautiful fey creature before him. He walked up the petals and stepped into a small pool of liquid. The woman was up to her knees in the pool and Arleith noticed he was only up to his ankles. It was something to note, but it still didn't matter as he reached to cup her face in his hands.

Pip looked as though she was mouthing 'this is for your own good' as she drew one of the two sais that she carried. Arleith turned his head towards her, trying to understand what was happening. He was confused, unable to comprehend why Pip would attack him or why he felt as if he had nothing to worry about ever again. Everything still felt as if he were looking through rippling water, but in that moment, things started to clear up. As if she were moving in slow motion, Arleith watched Pip go to stab him in the arm. His attention was pulled away and the rest of the world grew foggy again as a delicate hand reached out and touched his face, gently turning him back to stare deep into the creature's eyes again.

Without even looking like she knew Pip was there, a thick vine slammed into the small dragonborn's chest from the base of the plant that was covered by the open petals. The younger ranger went flying, nearly dropping her weapon as she landed heavily on the ground. Now

within proximity, the other creatures reached towards her with vines of their own. Winded from her landing, Pip had only just reoriented herself when she felt a firm tug on her ankle. Quick hands and thinking saved her as she drew her other sai and stabbed them both into the ground. With the added benefit of the prongs in her weapons, she managed to keep herself from being dragged. Straining as it pulled on her, she was surprised she managed to keep the upper hand in the precarious tug-o-war. It was short lived as it lifted her straight up instead, dislodging any grip she had.

The vines didn't seem to have enough strength to keep her aloft for long as it came crashing back down to the ground, still gripping her tightly. Scrambling, the small dragonborn hacked at the tendril dragging her across the ground. It was difficult since her weapon was more for stabbing than slashing, but she saw that she was making progress with the clear, sappy material seeping from the vine. She was still calling out to Arleith, hoping to get through to him. He still remained aware she was nearby and saying something, but his rapt attention was only for the pale green fey before him. She was so welcoming, so inviting, it felt like all of his troubles were distant memories long faded as he looked into her eyes. He reached out to caress her cheek, which she leaned towards as if a lover he hadn't seen in a long time.

He paused, just out of reach of her touch and slowly withdrew his hand. "Why am I doing this…? You're not Frostbite…"

Her expression changed from longing and comforting to immeasurable disdain and in that moment, Arleith's senses came rushing back with crystal clarity. He had just enough time to grab one of his tomahawks, throwing it behind him towards Pip, before the basin of the pool opened up. The sudden drop and pressure from the suction dragged him immediately into the bottom of wherever it drained to. Inside what he could only compare to a pitcher plant, he was completely submerged in a sickly sweet smelling nectar. The strange lighting from the sunless sky seemed to shine through enough to provide enough of a glow to give some sight. He saw the base of where the creature's legs fused with the plant and a small crease where the entrance had been sealed. Holding his breath, he pushed off the bottom and tried to pry it back open with his claws. He struggled for a few moments before the clear nectar started clouding pink in front of him. While his mind had been cleared instantly, the numbness in the rest of his body was a bit slower to recover, but it was starting now. His eyes began to burn, as did the insides of his nostrils. It started creeping all over his body when he realized what was happening. The pink was blood. Blood coming from his eyes as they burned in the acid this flower creature intended to digest him with. He screamed through his teeth, losing precious air as the pain wracked his body. Grabbing one of his daggers, he began slashing at the lid of the pitcher structure, but the material was so thick it wasn't doing much.

Topside, despite having only a fraction of a second to glance at Pip, Arleith's tomahawk flew in a perfect arc, landing and severing the vine around her ankle. With the moment of freedom, she snatched up the weapon. Hacking at one that was creeping towards her wrist, she tumbled back and turned a roll into a chance to spring to her feet. Sprinting at the one that had swallowed Arleith into her roots, she began casting a spell. Vines were closing in around her, but without

breaking eye contact with the creature she faded into a cloud of pink mist, rematerializing over her. Pip let the claws of her feet dig into the flowery creature's belly and gripped her shoulder with one hand, gouging deep into the flesh. Already shocked by such a bold move, the fey woman paled and shrank from the visage bearing directly into her face.

Pip dug her claws deeper, brandishing the tomahawk beneath the woman's chin. The quick incantation she had cast on herself took effect and her face became a pale mask, carved of petrified wood. As she spoke, the mouth of the mask curled and stretched farther back than it should, echoing in what seemed to be at least four different voices. Her dead, empty eyes with amethyst gems set into the sockets bore deep into the woman as the swirling symbols etched on the surface started to glow an ominous green.

"Release him to me, or be consumed by an agent of The Queen of Air and Darkness! Death is but a mercy granted to those who slight me!"

The plant woman was so terrified, both by the visage and the dangerous proximity of her that it took her a moment to respond. Dumbfounded, she gaped at the dragonborn until she curled her claws, digging them deeper into the creature's flesh. Shivering in fear, she opened the thick leaf that acted as a trap door under the surface of the nectar. Arleith's eyes were shut tight, but he could tell that light was shining on his face again. He reached out and clawed his way to the fresh air he desperately needed. With a gasp, he couldn't haul himself out any more than he had, the acid burning him into a state of painful numbness. Pip eyed the surroundings and saw that vines were coming for them again while the woman she was perched on was beginning to close the petals around them. She dropped down and grabbed Arleith by the weapon belts. Instead of pulling him though, she muttered another incantation and just as the trap door opened again to suck them both down into the digestive chamber. The two of them faded into pink mist just as all closed around them.

Pip could only hold such a spell a limited distance and her body was fatigued from doing it twice, but she managed to get them far enough away from the plant women and much closer to the river. They reappeared not ten feet from the riverbank as the illusion of the mask faded from her face. Arleith was shaking, the acid still burning him and making his muscles seize up so that he couldn't even move. Pip took out her waterskin and poured it over Arleith's face first, hoping to save his eyes. She tossed it aside when it was empty and readjusted her grip on the dagger belts. Heaving as best she could, the tiny dragonborn managed to inch the much larger ranger to the water. Dunking him completely, she tried to make it go faster by scraping what she could from his body with her claws.

"Open your eyes!" she pleaded in a shrill state of panic. "We've got to wash them out!"

Arleith tried, but the corrosive material combined with the agony made it impossible. Recovering the motor function of his arms, he reached to his face and pried his eyes open, holding his head underwater. When the pain was no longer building and he could keep his eyes open, Arleith

collapsed on the bank with Pip following suit. They both lay there next to each other, breathing heavily for a while until their heart rates went back down and they could breathe easily.

"What in the Nine Hells were those things?" Arleith finally asked. "Alraune," Pip let out a long breath.
"Seelie or Unseelie?"

"Neither," Pip said, then added, "but created by Unseelie."

"We should move and camp for a bit," Arleith groaned as he continued to lie still.
"They can't reach us," Pip assured him.
"Yeah, but I'm tempted to burn them," Arleith growled.

Pip frowned and looked him intently in the face. "Whatever you saw, whatever you felt, that's just what they do so that they can eat. They weren't real feelings."

Arleith turned to look at her in turn, but she turned her face once they made eye contact, so he rested his head again. "I don't like how real it felt."

"It's not fair to be so hard on yourself," Pip hugged her knees and began rocking back and forth. "Wizards use that pollen in love potions. It's just what it's meant to do. And hey! You snapped out of it on your own!"

Arleith heard her, but couldn't accept it. Seething with himself for not realizing what was happening sooner, not able to break free until it was practically too late, it was hard for him to think that he hadn't failed his goal in some way. He ground his jaw together, internally admonishing himself. Pip seemed to be getting nervous and agitated, which only frustrated him more. He was expecting some sort of outburst of chaotic energy for her to try and break the tension and he was in no mood for it. He was almost startled then, when instead his brooding was broken by a gentle hand on his shoulder and a soft voice filled with concern and care.

"Tell me about when you fell in love with Frostbite. I'm sure when you think about it, you'll know what you really feel."

Arleith shifted uncomfortably before sitting up with a groan. "C'mon Pip, you know neither of us is good with sharing our feelings."

"We can make it a game," Pip smiled, her voice still calmer but her smile returning. "We can trade questions. I'll ask one, then you ask one, and we do that until we can't think of anything."

Arleith grumbled, but if she was taking such a different approach from her usual self,

A Tale From the Argentum Bastian

he knew she was trying. "Fine. What do you want to know?"

"When did you fall in love with Frostbite?" Pip phrased her previous statement into her first question.

Arleith looked down and thought for a while before finally saying,"I don't know…"
"Oh come on!" Pip whined.
"I really don't," he insisted. "But I do know how." Pip scooted closer and stared at him earnestly.
Arleith shook his head and sighed. "It was because of you, in a way. When you disappeared she marched right up to the Kresh Mother and insisted she join the search party. Nothing anyone said could change her mind. No matter what, she would stubbornly say 'She's my cousin. I have to find her' or 'She's family. I have to save her'. That was the first time I noticed her for who she really was. We were just kids, so I wouldn't call it love then, but it was the first time I realized she wasn't just some spoiled brat. Everyone always fawned over her because of how big she was, how strong she was going to be, but you were all she cared about then. She and your sister even tried sneaking out when the adults wouldn't let them come along. She kept at it every day until you were brought home.

I started at the military academy shortly after that and didn't really think about her for a while. Then they told me that I was going to help with forest and fey survival training and there she was. Just as tall and powerful as everyone predicted. My guess was that the attention would have gotten to her head by then, so when she was assigned to me, I told myself I'd go hard on her because no one else would. Damn was I wrong. She worked so hard, all day, every day.
She didn't just accept that she was as amazing as everyone said. If anything, that made her work harder, like she was trying to earn that place. To live up to it. I couldn't help but admire her after that week of training. We started spending time together outside of the academy.
Eventually a lot. Somewhere along the way, my admiration became something else."

The stiffness in his voice that he started with had softened towards the end as memories of their younger days drifted through his mind. In maybe a dozen years, those fond moments hadn't faded. They brought a warmth and comfort to him that seemed to allow him to stop being angry with himself. There were many more details that he had glossed over, like the late nights they had spent under the stars together after sneaking out, the extra training she asked for but didn't really need, keeping items from each other just to have the excuse to bring them back to the other. When had they started flirting? It had felt so natural, so welcome, like they had always been that way.

Strawberries and Stones

Pip gave a wistful sigh and a smile with her normal energy back. "Okay, your turn!"

"I'm going to be nice and start easy on you," Arleith smirked, toying with the dagger that didn't match his set. "Why do you call Frostbite your sister?"

"Oh!" Pip laughed dismissively. "My mom and dad both died before I was old enough to leave the Kresh. Snapdragon and I were supposed to go live with Uncle Rotta'ghan and Frostbite. He died too though, so when I was brought home, it was to Frostbite and Snapdragon. I guess it felt less sad to think that I grew up with my sisters, that way only two people were dead, not four."

"I guess that wasn't as easy as I thought it was going to be," Arleith muttered. "But wait, they would have started at the academy…"

"One year after I was taken out of the Kresh," Pip finished for him.

"Didn't you try talking with the Kresh Mother? There's no way she would have let you grow up alone!" Arleigh felt his heart drop as the realization dawned on him.

Pip was quiet for a moment before she spoke again. "I tried to, but every time I visit, she gets sad. So I stopped bothering her."

The Kresh Mother, I'rosha, was the one solely responsible for the care of young dragonborn. From the time an egg was laid, to its hatching, and until the child was ten years old, she was their constant caretaker. Pip's disappearance would have felt like a personal failure. If she had kept her distance from the Kresh Mother and her sister and cousin had been required to start their academy training then Pip had basically grown up alone since she was eleven years old. A pit grew in Arleith's stomach as he came to that conclusion and he knew there was nothing that could be said or done that would mean anything compared to the life of solitude she had lived in a clan that said they cared for their own above all else.

"My turn again! I get two because you didn't wait your turn on your second one," Pip said, back to her normal self with complete indifference. "Why am I the only one that uses your nickname?"

Arleith went to argue, but stopped himself with a sigh. She had likely kept track or counted something he had said rather than considering it a continuation of the conversation which still made her technically right. "You know I can't answer that. I have no control over what people choose to call me."

A Tale From the Argentum Bastian

"I think it's because secretly everyone respects you a lot," Pip said, matter-of-factly. "Kind of like how no one calls my sister Snapdragon. It's always Praetora, or B'lanna. Or Preatora B'lanna! But that's so weird since we all get our nicknames first."

It was an odd topic to fixate on, but Arleith had to admit it was also a valid point. "Maybe that's something you could change. I don't think anyone in the clan thinks like you. Maybe we need things to be different."

"Eww! I'd be stuck talking to boring, stuffy people all the time!" Pip wretched. "Not even over my dead body!"

Arleith laughed, a deep, pleasant sound that seemed to even light Pip up more than usual. "Alright, second question."

"Have you really never seen any of the Fey before?" Pip asked with genuine disbelief.

"I'm familiar with a few in the forest around home," Arleith shrugged. "Met a treant while I was on patrol, there's a couple dryads I say hello to once in a while. I usually take a few minutes to talk to them every time I'm out."

"No fair!"Pip gasped. "They never talk to me!"

Arleith shrugged again, this time apologetically. "Maybe it's just because you're busy. They're not really the type to play. I literally just say 'hi' and ask them how they're doing. Sometimes they don't even come out. They like it when the forest is peaceful."

"Fine!" Pip sighed. "I guess that's okay then. Your turn again!"

Arleith considered a moment before he said, "Okay, my next question… Why did you really want to come along? With me, here, I mean."

Pip's demeanor shifted almost instantly. She was somber, distant, and when she spoke it was almost as if it were a different person. "My sisters never smile. I can't remember the last time they smiled. Anyone that says they've seen them smile doesn't know what a real one looks like. I've tried… so hard… but I'm nothing but trouble. Everyone wants me to go away. I just make things worse. But I can't go away. Not until they smile again. Neither of them has been happy… until you. Frostbite came home one night, and there it was… A real smile. I didn't believe it at first, but it came back every day. You are the only one who has made her happy for as long as I can remember… And I hate you for it… But I love you for it… But I hate you for it…"

Arleith felt his throat choke as she started sobbing, heavy tears rolling down her face. He hesitated to comfort her, unsure if it would be welcome. He settled on tentatively putting a hand on her little shoulder. She turned and hugged him, burying her face in his chest, bawling and shaking as she held him as tightly as her tiny frame could. Arleith gingerly held her, silently letting her let out everything she had kept inside for who could guess how long. It had always been easy to forget that she wasn't a child. She was so small and so childishly energetic. With how carefree she was, it was also easy to forget that there were few in the clan that had it as rough as she did, including her cousin.

"I was supposed to fix everything," Pip finally sniffled when she had nothing left. "If it's going to be you though, then I at least wanted to know that I helped."

Arleith squeezed her a little tighter, the soothing tenor of his voice reassuring her as best he could. "You've been a great help. I'd be dead or lost, or hell, still even looking for this place if it weren't for you. I've always been glad you're around, so I know your sisters are too."

Pip stayed there, quiet but slowly quit trembling. Finally pulling back to sit again, she wiped her face. "You're wet."

Arleith grinned, glancing at her drenched clothes and armor from the river, both of them soaked from their tangle with the alraune. "So are you."

She gave a short laugh, wiping her face again. "This game is stupid." "We can play it any time you want."
Pip nodded, her eyes still directed at the ground. "Still a dangerous offer." "Still willing to take my chances," Arleith said with a smile.
They breathed easy a moment before moving upstream to set up camp. They were quiet the entire time, but there was no tension in the air. While they were cold blooded and didn't need the warmth, they started a fire to dry out their clothes so that they wouldn't risk getting scale rot. They spent the time before they slept treating their armor and oiling their weapons. Arleith did a quick inventory of what they had left. The digestive fluid from the alraune didn't seem to affect other plant-like material, so the flower crown Pip had made was surprisingly unscathed, but the seals on the jars of honey and cream had been dissolved and the contents ruined. All of the rations they packed were practically sludge, leaving them with nearly nothing.

"Here, eat this," Pip handed Arleith a strawberry. "It'll keep us from starving, but it's

A Tale From the Argentum Bastian

not going to be very satisfying."

Arleith took the single berry and examined it before popping it into his mouth. "You know, I never learned this spell. They didn't offer it at the academy."

As he swallowed it down, he could feel it nourishing his body in an instant, but Pip was right, it wasn't very satisfying to an empty stomach.

"Yuck! school!" Pip faked gagging. "I can't believe they made me go! How does anyone sit still that long? So boring!"

Arleith chuckled as he closed his eyes to sleep. Pip curled up nearby and was quickly asleep, breathing softly. Sleep didn't come to Arleith as quickly as he mulled over everything that had happened. They had already spent a week looking for the Feywild, and it was impossible to tell how long they had been inside the realm. People were going to start noticing though, if they

hadn't already. While he knew the gemstones in the faerie's domain were supposed to be extravagant, he hadn't anticipated it would take this long to find a location to look. Thoughts tumbling in his head, he finally fell into a restless sleep.

The two of them broke camp wordlessly the following morning, though Pip hummed to herself and skipped alongside Arleith when they moved out. Both of them sore and starting to get worn out, they mostly got by on determination alone. They made good progress, closing the range to the mountain significantly by the time the sky decided to dim.

The mountain itself was not nearly as welcoming as they thought it would be once they got closer. It was still almost completely crystalline, just in a raw form. The formations made by the multitude of shimmering stones looked far more sinister than they had guessed from a distance. Spires like needle teeth jutted out of the ground, staying in dark colors despite how the light reflected through the prisms. It washed out the area in a dull, purple-black light and entering its shadow offered an unwelcoming chill to the air. To their relief though, there were raw gems in the riverbed that were suitable size.

"Not that I don't think Frostbite deserves the best, but that mountain is giving me the creeps," Pip shuddered.

"Same. Let's check the area here first before moving on," Arleith agreed. "I think it's best we don't grab anything extra either. We don't have enough to leave in exchange."

Strawberries and Stones

Wading to the center, they picked up anything that glittered beneath the surface. There was an abundance of quartz in colors neither of them had seen before, amethysts bigger than their fists and even sapphires the size of drake eggs. Arleith let them all go as he sifted through the soft sand. While the quartz might have been a good choice for the unusual colors, he still couldn't help but feel if he kept looking he would find something truly special. Pip spent most of her time chasing fish, insisting that Arleith had to find the right one by himself. She caught a couple frogs as well and was otherwise splashing about and having fun.

He tried several spots, inching closer and closer to the shadow of the mountain. About the time he was about to ask Pip how she felt about getting closer to the mountain, a paler stone caught his eye, mostly buried by silt and sapphires. He carefully dug it out and washed it before examining it in the light. It was a piece of iolite, roughly the size and shape of a pear. It was a pale, lavender colored stone that almost seemed to glow depending on how the light caught it. He had never seen a gem that color before and it didn't take him long to decide that it was exactly what he was looking for.

"Hey, Pip," he said quietly, still examining it as he walked it over to his friend, "I think I found it." "I think I did too!" she shouted back, holding up a frog.

As they waded toward each other to show off their finds a thin wall of water separated them, splashing them both. Arleith shook the water off of his face and looked over at Pip in confusion. She shrugged back, but as she did, a dark line of blood appeared at a weak point in her armor and began seeping heavily. Arleith immediately dropped the gem he was carrying and rushed to her side.

"Are you okay?" he asked sternly.

Pip was already applying pressure to the wound with a healing touch and winced. "It's fine. I'm fine."

The two of them honed their focus and scanned the area. They were both familiar with the type of resonance fey creatures made in the living world. Combined with magically enhancing their senses for a moment, Arleith saw tracks on the shore. Tiny footprints in the soft dirt by the edge of the river and how fast the creatures were moving gave him an educated guess of what had burst through the area.

"Quicklings," he growled, standing back to back with Pip.

"Ugh," Pip sighed in disgust as she drew her sais. "Unseelie tattletales."

A Tale From the Argentum Bastian

They were still, trying to catch any signs of movement. While they only saw the grass rustle as if being blown by the wind, they were surrounded by echoing giggles. Arleith heard them coming first, but he was still too slow to move as something streaked past them. Moving fast enough to run across the water were several blue skinned, humanoid creatures. Like pixies without wings and far more malicious, they cut past them, kicking up more water. Pip coughed, making Arleith turn out of concern. It didn't sound like she got water up her nose but more like a throat injury. His eyes widened as his assessment was confirmed. Pip had dropped a sai and was clutching her neck, the pink mist that surrounded her hand whenever she cast magic almost drowned out by a gout of blood from a deep wound she was trying to heal.

"Behind you!" she choked.

Arleith spun around, zeroing in on two more coming up behind him. His reflexes were fast, but not as fast as the creatures. He threw two daggers the quicklings easily ran around. He braced for impact, unable to draw more before they got there. Instead, they arced around him, each one stabbing Pip in a thigh before streaking off again. While Pip was healing her wounds, she staggered, her scales losing luster rapidly.

"S-Spire… I'm not fine," she murmured as she collapsed into the river.

Arleith wrapped an arm around her waist before she completely dropped. The wounds she had were starting to ooze black as she went limp. He had smelt such ichorous poisons before, usually made in the bogs and fens of the Feywild and used by the most devious of the Unseelie

that wandered the Dreaming Grove. Casting a spell to draw out the poison, he hurried to shore. He could hear the approach of the quicklings again, but there was little he could do while carrying Pip. Again they avoided him and made slashes at the smaller dragonborn. He finished expelling the poison for Pip's body, but her condition didn't improve. Rushing her to their campsite, he laid her on the ground and examined her wounds. He felt his anger building as he looked at the gashes all over her body. There were at least two other types of poison in her system by the way her injuries reacted to them. He could only axtract one at a time, but at least it would slow the others down too. He gathered as much magical energy in his hands as he could, pushing it into Pip's body. As if being stitched by threads of spider silk, all of her wounds closed and sealed, bringing her out of danger of bleeding out.

With a snarl, he drew his tomahawks and stood over her protectively. Waiting for the quicklings to return didn't take long. He counted six streaks closing in on them, but instead of getting a better vantage on them and giving away that he was aware of

"

them, he stood his ground.
Something he was counting on was that they didn't know that he had boobytrapped their camp the night before. The magic hadn't faded yet, and they would have to cross them to get to Pip.

As predicted, they dashed right for them. An explosion from the ground had darts he had planted chasing them down. More sporadic than a thrown weapon, they chased their quarry, causing the quicklings to veer wildly, only to trigger more of them. Arleith used their confusion as an opportunity to throw his tomahawks into the mix, narrowly missing. Knowing he had pressure on the quicklings, his hands moved fluidly, drawing daggers and throwing them as fast as the creatures could move. He finally caught the break he needed when one triggered one of his snares as it tried to escape the cordon he had set.

"Enough of this," Arleith muttered, drawing one of the concealed needles from his bracers.

As he twirled it around one finger, magic writing etched itself onto the side, looking as though it had been written in shadow before he threw it and the one suspended in the air. The moment it impacted the creature, the needle exploded in a hail of shrapnel, killing it instantly and maiming several of the others.Two more were killed with daggers to their hearts before they even realized what was happening. Arleith marched towards the rest, watching them scramble to escape. The only one left uninjured took off as he stooped to pick up one of his tomahawks, whispering another word of magic, tying a thread only he could see from his wrist to the retreating quickling. Facing forward, he threw it to his right, intercepting one that was looping around towards Pip, cutting clean through the neck and lodging into a tree. The headless body tumbled to a halt, going several more feet due to the speed the creature had been running. The last one still present was too injured to run, dragging its body across the grass in what must have been an agonizingly slow pace for it. Arleith stepped down and pressed hard on one of its injured legs. Satisfied it wouldn't escape, he looked up again. Scanning the area, he caught a glimpse of the thread connected to the last. Drawing a javelin from the carrier on his back, Arleith hefted it only once. Throwing it in an impressive arc, it flew faster than even the creatures could run. It pierced through the quickling's back, pinning it to the ground still standing, dead in an instant.

Silently, Arleith bent down, picking up his captive by the neck. It started chittering at him, the expression on its face suggesting it was trying to talk its way into mercy. Arleith didn't understand Sylvan, so he tilted his head as he considered his options. He was furious, but it didn't often show with an explosive temper like most people. The Sivak's blood all ran cold and Arleith was in no mood for mercy. They had assaulted Pip, unprovoked as far as he was concerned. They had used no less than three, and maybe more poisons on her. For some reason they wanted her dead. There was no way for him to get information from it, as much as he wanted to know why.

Eventually, he reached for a vial he saw attached to the quickling's belt. He popped the cork and sniffed it. As suspected, no self respecting assassin would use a poison without carrying an antidote in case of an accident or a bribe. He stared the writhing creature down in his grip, waiting for it to make eye contact with him. Fey creatures hated making eye contact unless they were the ones that ate flesh, and those were the ones you didn't want to meet. The midnight blue skin made a pair of bright yellow eyes stand out, with only a pupil to break up the color.
Wild, electric blue hair was permanently swept back, tapering to a long point from how fast the little creatures could run. Barely three feet tall, spindly and frail looking, few would guess how dangerous quicklings were. And even with that, they were still mostly just messengers to older, darker, more powerful fey. When it did finally look him in the eyes and saw the intent in the dragonborn, it struggled harder to break free. Arleith snapped its neck in his claws by merely tightening his grip. A soft crunch and the quickling went limp. He tossed the body aside as if discarding an apple core before walking back over to Pip.

Still seething, he cradled Pip's head and coaxed the antidote down her throat. He managed to get her to swallow it all and began focusing all the magical energy he had left in him to try and neutralize the last of the poison in her body. It had been a while since he'd gone all out on an enemy and if he hadn't been so worried for Pip he might have thought it felt good to unleash everything on someone after his months of stress. Instead he watched Pip as she lay there, making sure her breathing never slowed.

After several hours, she finally stirred with a groan. "Go to sleep, you're creeping me out."

As if the tension were cut by a knife, Arleith's face split into a smile and he couldn't help but chuckle. That chuckle grew into a full blown laugh. He laughed hard enough for Pip to open one eye and giggle herself. It truly was infectious, as she weakly laughed with him once she got going too, clutching her freshly healed throat once in a while to prevent herself from coughing. When it started to die down, Pip saw Arleith wipe his face and take a deep breath. The tears she pretended not to see were not from how hard they had been laughing, but fear and relief.
She smiled to herself and curled up more comfortably, drifting back to sleep. Arleith watched her rest, determined to make sure nothing happened while she slept. He didn't have enough left to set up more magic traps since he hadn't put a large amount of focus on it at the academy. With the already set ones spent, it was back to the

classic watch shifts.

In the tall weeds by the edge of the river, soft lights started drifting from the cattail blades. They continued to spread, giving off a soft glow that Arleith assumed were fireflies. He only started to question it when they were close enough for him to notice that they were a lot larger than he thought. Much larger than any normal insect he had seen. Before he could redraw his conclusion, he began to feel his head droop and his eyelids get heavy. As much as he fought it, he fell asleep sitting up, almost positive he heard soft singing on the breeze.

Arleith woke with a start as he realized he was sleeping. He hadn't wanted to leave Pip unattended and felt his heart skip a beat when he wondered how long he'd been asleep. A quick scan relaxed him as he saw Pip laying exactly where he had left her, though sprawled out instead of being in a tight little ball. Another quick look around and he noticed that all of the weapons he had thrown were neatly lined up in front of him, clean of blood and ready to be put away. The bodies of the quicklings were all gone and again he felt the discomfort of the ease faeries had doing as they pleased. Grateful whatever had come out seemed to be benevolent, he began sheathing his weapons.

"That was very generous," he said softly, both unsure if he was heard by whoever or whatever had done this was nearby, and not wanting to wake Pip if he could help it.

As he put his weapons away, he noticed an amber substance on his bracers and the front of his armor. Taking a few quick scratches at it, he realized it was dried sap. He looked around again, confused when he didn't see any nearby trees. He decided that it was probably some joke he didn't understand, he figured he would just wash it off in the river. Remaining where he was for the time being, Arleith waited for Pip to wake on her own. He wasn't sure how much residual damage was left from the poisons, but she needed to rest. She stirred not long after he had finished putting his weapons away, the shimmering butterflies hovering around her fluttering away as she sat up and stretched. Arleith had to stop and stare, rubbing his eyes to make sure he wasn't seeing things.

"Your sister is going to kill me."

"Why? What did you do?" Pip asked as she finished a big yawn.

"Well… nothing but," Arleith hesitated. "You've got a little extra decoration on your head."

Pip reached up and felt around, eventually grabbing onto her horns. Only, they weren't so much horns anymore. They had split and started growing without metallic color. While they had slept, Pip's horns had grown out into antlers, both relatively short ones that had two prongs each. With a look of shock and a squeal of delight, she rushed to the river to look at herself in the reflection of the water. Arleith joined her, watching the smaller dragonborn tug on them as she bounced with excitement.

"Aren't I cute!" she shrieked. "Wow! I can't believe it! I'm going to show everyone!"

Knowing it would be something she couldn't easily hide, Arleith simply nodded. "Suits you, but I think I'm going to be in trouble."

He had heard of those that had been exposed to enough Fey magic they began to take on similar physical traits. There were even records of others in the clan that had their horns grow into ram's horns, some sprouted gossamer wings that couldn't lift them but were still beautiful, and some that just had a fragrance to them like cinnamon or nutmeg. It shouldn't have surprised him that it would eventually happen to Pip, but he was fairly certain that since it happened on his watch, he would be held responsible. The concern melted away a bit as his thoughts trailed to his mother. She had also been similarly spiky, like him, with the numerous long scales that mimicked hair. He had always thought that hers looked a little more like vines and her spurs more like thorns. She had also been a bit of an odd one in the clan, but it hadn't been as taboo as it was for Pip. From what he had understood, most people figured she had experienced something traumatic as a cadet, but no one had really filled in the details, not really wanting to make her relive it. Whenever he had asked, she would just smile and say that the faeries had taught her magic to help her survive and wouldn't elaborate more. Were she still around though, he figured Pip would have liked his mother. At least neither of them would have been lonely.

"I love them!" Pip said as she turned her head to look at herself at different angles. "I promise I won't let my family think it's your fault! I didn't know I'd get a present too!"

Arleith patted her on the back before going around her to the shore. "Hate to disrupt the view, but I have something I need to get."

Wading back into the river, he tried to get his bearings on where he was when the quicklings attacked. He washed his armor of the sap quickly before focusing on what was really important. Moving carefully and slowly, he scanned for the iolite that he had found earlier. As if sensing the mood, the river didn't shimmer or shine at all. The sapphires and amethyst that had sparkled so bright before were dull and look barely more than plain rocks. Pip stopped playing with her new antlers and looked over at him. She was quiet and surprisingly still for several minutes, watching him.

"I'm glad you like me enough to drop something so important…" Pip murmured. "I hope it's not lost."

Arleith had to stop and look at her intently for such an uncharacteristically meek statement. She had her head hung low and she was wringing her hands as if she were ashamed.

"Come on, Pip, you know your life is more important than some rock."

She turned so much that her back was almost to him, her tone not the least bit lifted. "But that's why we came here. So that you could propose to Frostbite. And now it's lost because of me. I told you I'm nothing but trouble."

"Pip, listen up, because I'm only going to say this once," Arleith said sternly. "If you think for a second that I would consider this a success if I went home with the perfect Tlhogh Stone but lost you along the way, then I have failed you as a friend."

Pip swayed shyly. "We're really friends?"

Arleith nodded sagely. "After what we've been through on this trip, I would trust you with my life." Pip's face slowly turned to a heartfelt smile. "I've never had a dragonborn friend before."
"It's an honor to be the first," Arleith tilted his head as if to bow. "Everyone else is missing out."

They gave each other a slight nod before Arleith went back to searching the riverbed. Pip stayed on shore, keeping a lookout for any potential danger while his focus was downward. In just the right lighting when a cloud shifted to make the sky more orange and pink, the gem Arleith had found finally revealed itself for the second time. Gently picking it up as if he still couldn't believe he'd found it at all, including the first time, he waded back to shore staring at it. Pip came over to inspect the pale gemstone for herself.

"To think, drow and duergar kill each other over pieces barely big enough to set in a ring," Arleith said under his breath, "and I'm holding one as big as my fist."

"Frostbite is going to love it," Pip said in awe as she got to look at it for the first time. "What shape are you going to make?"

Arleith looked at it for a while. Even the shape was perfect for what he had in mind.

A Tale From the Argentum Bastian

"Whenever I ask her about what it was like being a paladin, most of it goes over my head. But the thing that always sticks out is that she talks about how she's tasked with protecting and nurturing the light in everyone around her. I thought I might modify a teardrop shape cut to look like a candle flame."

Pip leaned over and looked at it more carefully, eying up the shape this time. "It looks almost like that's what it wants to be turned into."

Arleith hesitated a moment, then asked with uncertainty, "Do you think she'll like it?" Pip looked up at him and smiled. "Spire?"
"Yeah?" "You're stupid."
His chuckle drifted into a sigh. He had never felt so nervous before, but he wasn't going to let that stop him. The two of them sat there in silence, admiring the stone as Arleith rotated it in his

palm. With steeled resolve, he gently wrapped it in a bandana and carefully placed it in his satchel.

"Let's go home," Arleith nodded, starting the trek downstream.

The walk back seemed to move a lot faster than it took to get there. Before long, they were already back in the tall plains again. They took turns sleeping, fresh out of ways to appease any fey creature they crossed paths with. With days being impossible to separate, they still had to guess they were making better time than they had.

Eventually they made it back to the edge of the bog that the river flowed into. Neither of them spoke it out loud, but this was the first thing that seemed truly different on the way back. There were more dead trees than before, twisted and gnarled in different shapes. Arleith couldn't help but think to himself that they looked like they had died in agony. The entire forest felt like it was watching them, but whatever unseen eyes were on them kept their distance. The air was musty and heavy, bringing a layer of dread to the original foreboding that was present before. Arleith and Pip managed to convince themselves it was just in their minds. It didn't stop either of them from having a ready hand on a weapon, just in case.

It wasn't overly oppressive after a while to the two dragonborn until they started to smell rotting meat in the wind. It wasn't overt at first, but it grew stronger as they walked. It didn't seem to matter what direction they turned, it was getting stronger as if it were following them. They started to move faster to try and get away from whatever it might be, but it lingered and grew more and more. With the faintest crack of a branch that was too close for comfort, Arleith grabbed Pip and ducked behind a set of twisting roots from a fallen tree. Pip didn't even struggle, despite having his hand clamped over her muzzle. They both waited and looked around, listening for anything that might be coming.

While the stench stayed relatively put for a moment, long, pale fingers curled over the set of roots. Frost began collecting around these fingers that cracked and popped like the snapping of ice whenever they moved. The very air around them seemed to plummet in temperature, so much so that even the silver dragonborn were chilled. It was getting almost unbearably cold for them until they started hearing the slight sound of sniffing above them. A long, crooked nose came over the roots above them, the nostrils flaring with each sharp inhale, like a hunting dog snuffling the trail of a fox. A head began to peer over and looking up they locked eyes with a withered old woman, her skin blue, lips cracked and split from the extreme cold coming from her body. She kept sniffing, despite staring directly at them, leaving Arleith to wonder why she hadn't done anything yet. Arms too long hoisted a thin body up and then Arleith noticed why she hadn't attacked. Her eyes had flat, uneven surfaces. They were frozen and useless in the body of what could only be a hag. What didn't fit was why it was here. Arleith had seen one before, the same icy presence, the same eyes, the same cracking limbs. These types of hags lived in the coldest of mountains and tundras, commanding wendigos and devouring the flesh of any lost wanderer unfortunate enough to cross their path.

"Mahrow! Stop chasing the wind!" a shrill old woman's voice cut through the air as if she were screaming right next to the dragonborn.

The hag above them hissed, her voice garbled and low as if she weren't speaking with her mouth, but her throat. "If it weren't for your stench, I'd have found something to eat by now. If you get into the coven, I may kill you myself so that I don't starve. There is something near that is needed."

"You've been moaning about that for days. Why are you so intent on this?"

The hag's head lowered, her wispy white hair dangling just far enough to move with each shallow breath the two dragonborn took. Her sightless eyes scanned the area with a long exhale of breath that smelled of drying blood.

"Something hidden is revealed. Moirai wants it found and broken. Those of dragon flesh may yet still have it."

"Ugh, not even their children are tender," the shrill voice whined. "Must we go there?"

There was a long pause before the hag slowly withdrew, her hollow, self echoing voice resonating still too close for comfort. "She who breaks it will be the new sister of her coven. We must hurry before more come to find it."

There was more snapping and crunching of limbs as the hag crawled away on all fours like a scurrying spider through the thicket. It and the stench slowly faded, but neither Sivak dared move until they were completely gone. Arleith slowly released his grip on Pip, feeling sluggish, his muscles stiff from the tense moment combined with the chilled air.

"What would we have? Is it the gem?" Pip whispered.

"I don't think so," Arleith shook his head. "They were talking about the kreshlings, which makes me think whatever they're talking about would be in the Argentum Bastian."

"What makes you sure?" Pip asked, visibly shaking in fear.

"If they were talking about us, they wouldn't think about where we lived, only where we are," he reasoned. "We have to get back. We have to warn everyone."

Pip agreed and the two of them found their bearings. They ran as fast as they could, hoping they were properly backtracking their original path. They still followed the edge of the bog, but even more than before, the terrain seemed to have changed significantly in a short amount of time. More than once they slipped on a black substance that seemed to be degrading plant matter and more of the trees seemed to be dead. They were twisted and cracked much like the ones he'd seen earlier, but they also seemed to have a slight layer of frost on them. Looking

further ahead, it was fairly plain to see that there was a trail of the two types of destruction. The rotten, sludge-like trail veered off and disappeared into the bog, but the trail of ice seemed to be heading the same way they were.

They only stopped an hour at a time, catching enough of a breather to keep going. While Pip was able to keep producing berries to give them energy, both of them were starting to suffer for not eating a real meal. Eventually, the path did diverge from theirs, heading deed into the dead and gloomy forest just before they reached the path with the golden leaves. They skidded to a halt when Arleith's eye caught something he recognized as out of place.

Just off the path, there was a log covered in ice crystals, but what Arleith saw was the trail of disturbed leaves and dirt. Pip eyed him curiously when he went to inspect, but stayed a bit back to cover him from behind.

Strawberries and Stones

"It's a good log," Pip said as he inspected it closely.

"It's going to be okay," he whispered, turning it over. "I'm not going to hurt you."

He heard Pip leap back as the log turned over and a weak illusion faded away, turning a dryad face up. Her skin was a mossy green that carried lines that looked like the grain of wood, with long, thick green hair that flowed gracefully to her ankles. Her murky brown-black eyes were wide with terror, but she seemed to allow Arleith to gentle put a hand behind her shoulders to raise her head. She was severely injured, a shard of ice sticking out of her chest where her heart was. All of her joints, knees, elbows, wrists, even each individual knuckle, was slowly splitting open as ice crystals grew from inside her. It looked agonizing, bringing his thoughts back to the gnarled trees they'd seen earlier. His jaw tightened as he imagined what kind of cruelty it would take to kill a peaceful creature in such a way. His thoughts clearly brought an idea of exactly what would have done this to the girl in his arms.

"What's happening to her?" Pip sprang forward, searching her satchel for a medicine kit. "I don't know, but I think she bumped into our friend from the bog," Arleith muttered.
He scanned around the area while gingerly scooping the up dryad. There were several trees that had frost embedded in the bark around them. It took a moment, but his gaze finally fell on one in the direction the dryad had crawled from. A tree with several spears of ice piercing through it stood, still wilting as it slowly died. Watching the leaves brown and curl, the dryad's hair seemed to match, browning and turning brittle.

"She needs a new tree," Arleith looked up at Pip.

"What does that even mean?" Pip shrieked, trying to restore the dryad with her healing magic to no effect.

"She's a tree spirit and her tree is dying," Arleith stated. "She needs a new tree. Please tell me you've got some acorns or something in there."

Pip dumped her bag on the ground and frantically searched through the spilt contents. "How are you so calm? She's dying!"

Arleith could see the meadow they arrived in. They had to be close to the Rift they had come through. Just on the other side would be plenty of things they could use to save her. As much as the clan needed warning, he had never left anyone behind, stranger or friend. Pip's manic energy in her nervous state might be exactly what he needed if he could focus it.

"Grab the crown out of my bag," he said as he tried to do some quick calculations.

Pip grabbed one of the only two things left in Arleith's satchel and pulled out the crown she had made before they left. "You kept this?"

"It was well made," he said, carefully placing it on the dryad's head.

The braided stems seemed to reach out and attach to her hair and weave themselves in. Arleith let out a small breath of relief as the flower petals slowly began to wilt and curl instead of her hair progressing as it had. It would give them a little extra time, but it was impossible to tell how much. He reached out to Pip and put a calming hand on her shoulder.

"Listen to me. We're going to run back. You get through the Rift and find anything you can. Hazelnut, acorn, pinecone, any seed from a tree. I want you to go as fast as you can. When you find one, come back in and I'll meet you part way. I'll be carrying her, so I'll be behind, but I will be following you. Do you understand? Can you do this?"

Pip had been chewing on one of her claws nervously, and removed it so that she could answer. "Run through, get a tree seed, come back. Yes… yes I can do that."

Drawing some of his own magic, Arleith pushed a spell into Pip, invigorating her running speed. "Go! I'm right behind you!"

Like a bolt, she took off. To most passers by, she would have been nothing but a streak of silver and green as she reached the meadow and kept going. Arleith got to his feet, delicately doing his best not to hurt the wounded dryad further. Watching her face, he guessed which way to carry her would be most comfortable before following behind. Watching the flowers and tall grass part as if split by a stroke of wind, he could tell Pip was putting her all into her sprint on top of what he had imbued in her for a short while.

It was slower for Arleith, but he still made better time than many others would have. It took him almost an hour to reach the meadow, his muscles already burning from the way he and Pip had already been pushing themselves. At his current pace though, what had taken the two dragonborn a day to hike when they first arrived would only take a few hours. It was still far too long, but he pushed the thought out of his head, trying not to watch the flower petals on the crown wither away.

Strawberries and Stones

The flowers in the meadow closed when he passed, just like before, but he moved so quickly they started opening again before they even closed. All manner of small creatures darted away, just quick enough for him to not be able to see what they were. Glowing balls of light flew in every direction. Faeries didn't like being startled, but there was no time to consider that so long as he wanted to keep the dryad alive. Legs going numb and his arms straining, he saw Pip finally make it to the other side, where she disappeared from view.

It was enough motivation to keep him going and by the time he could see through the Rift, there was Pip, running back towards it. His breath ragged, he still managed to look down and reassure the dryad, 'We're going to make it! Hold on a couple more minutes!"

Pip was about to come back through, shouting unheard and waving a fistful of something Arleith couldn't make out when suddenly the ground shifted. The flowers of the meadow right at the Rift began to twist and grow, several shoving Pip back into Malgrave while getting taller, blocking off Arleith from getting through as well. An unseen force yanked the dryad from his grasp making him slide to a stop.

"Speak your name, dragonborn," an angry, feminine voice echoed throughout the valley.

As it did, a long, lavender robe seemed to materialize before him and an elegant mask, polished white and decorated with painted gold vines across the surface appeared at the shoulders. It was more of an elegant gown that seemed to flow around a delicate figure, with long, cascading hair that appeared blonde at first, but was a pale green in the light. All that he could see of her skin was her hands, far too slender to be a human's. It could have been an elf, but he had his doubts.

Arleith swallowed hard and gave the best bow he could with his aching body. "My friends and clan call me Spire-"

"Your real name, Sivak," the voice bellowed around him again, but with no indication from the mask or the woman's throat that she was actually speaking. "I am in no mood for games."

Arleith stood petrified for a moment. There was something more to this woman's presence that didn't feel like an ordinary Fey being. Much older, much more powerful. If she wished him harm, there would be nothing he could do about it. The same thought calmed him a bit. She could do it regardless of how he responded. This was a formality.

A Tale From the Argentum Bastian

"I am Sivak Arleith, son of Lethe and Arlas," he spoke clearly as he knelt, doing away with all theatrics in his speech.

The woman shifted slightly at that, almost as if surprised before the voice spoke again. "There are thieves disrupting my realm. You moved the riverbed! You take my stones, you frighten my people! And you have spilled blood! Now you take one of my dryads to freeze her heart!"

"I did all of that except the last," Arleith raised his head and slowly stood again. "My intention was to save her life."

"What is done cannot be undone. What makes you believe you can change fate, mortal?" and with that, she lowered the dryad from the sky, surrounded in a golden light and hovering between them.

"Something that was taught to me long ago was that a dryad could be saved by occupying a tree that had yet to grow," Arleith said, trying to keep his thoughts from straying towards who had told him this, but a mental image of his mother passed through his mind. "She would be the spirit of this new tree. Or am I wrong?"

Again there was a pause, the masked face tilting curiously at him. "You are not wrong, silver one. An admirable goal, but it does not make up for the damage that has been done before her finding."

"I didn't mean to cause harm and had brought gifts to offer for trade," he said. "I didn't know upsetting the river would offend you, but I will not apologize for defending myself or my friend from quicklings."

"I accept these," the woman said thoughtfully, "but you do not fully acknowledge your theft. Why do you want this gemstone?"

Arleith hesitated. Partially because a part of him didn't want to get personal with someone essentially holding him hostage until she was satisfied, partially because he didn't have a real argument to defend himself anymore. What he intended to do and what was actually done were very different, especially in the eyes of the Fey. He couldn't help but think of Gol'rotta. This was all for her, the stone was for her. Would the Fey woman let him go out of mercy just because-

"Marriage? Is that what I see?" she cut off his thoughts as she was reading them. Arleith nodded, but remained silent.
"I see now. Yes, that would make sense. And your treasures were lost, that much is true. You've been through a lot for this," she turned her hand so that her palm

was facing up, lifting the gem out of his satchel and raising the dryad higher again without touching anything. "Do you still think it was worth it?"

Arleith was sure she was trying to catch him on something, but he didn't feel like he was clever enough to figure out what it was. Was she hoping for hesitance? Regret that he hadn't done

something else, or found an easier stone to use? As with before he left, the only thing that would have made the journey not worth it was if Pip had died. She did come close, but she was okay. If anything, he had gained more than he thought he would have by making friends with Pip and getting a little insight into one of the greatest enigmas of the clan. Gol'rotta was worth any amount of hardship. He'd been a senior soldier working under a younger officer, always together but as far apart as possible. He'd accepted the risk of dishonor and exile when he left. There was no answer he wanted to give other than the honest one.

"Yes," he said firmly, looking directly into the eyes of the mask. "Wouldn't change a thing."

There was no way to see into the eyes of the mask, so they were little more than empty black slits to him. She did not look away like so many other Fey did, but Arleith didn't pick up anything sinister when she spoke. If anything, she sounded amused. "A bargain with you then, for your theft must not go unpunished. If this dragoness is so precious to you as to make you trespass and steal from me, then I will let you keep it. If she accepts your offering, then our wager is done. But, should she reject you, you will suffer greatly. Do we have a deal?"

Arleith grimaced as she reached out her dainty hand for him to shake. "Not thrilled about calling it a deal, but yes, I accept."

There was a soft, warm pulse of energy as their hands clasped together. She held him there a moment longer, stopping him from pulling away. Tattoos of brambles were woven across the back of her hand and up her arm that he hadn't noticed at their distance. Arleith recoiled as one of them snaked down her thumb and left the skin. Despite the almost fragile looking hand, he couldn't break her grip. Resigned to whatever happened, he relaxed as the thorn covered vine wrapped around his wrist several times. It began to tighten until it seemed to sink into and then past his bracer. It didn't cut or tear it, but simply went through as if they were immaterial. A slight tingling in his scales and suddenly it stopped. The woman let go and turned her left hand slowly downward again. The piece of iolite drifted back into his satchel and the dryad fell gently back into Arleith's arms.

A Tale From the Argentum Bastian

"You are free to go, Son of Lethe," the masked Fey said, turning and fading as if becoming invisible, but also sounding far away. "Take her with you, nurture her back to health. Your kindness to her will not be forgotten, and neither will our pact…"

There was a slight rumbling sound as the flowers blocking the entrance shrank back down to their regular size and settled back into the meadow. Pip ran through as soon as she fit, even riding a few of them in to try and move faster. As she thrust a hazelnut at him, Arleith could see that her hands were raw and bleeding as if she had been pounding on a wall. He took it and was about to thank her, when he caught himself.

"This is perfect. You're a great help."

Pip beamed at him as he put it up to the dryad's feeble hand. "You're finally getting it right!"

He flashed a quick smile before gently coaxing the dryad to switch over to the hazelnut. It didn't take as much persuasion as it did just trying to keep her lucid. She was fading fast, but once she was aware of them again and her only chance she gripped it tightly. There was a rush of green energy leaving her body and as it did so, her skin turned grey and brittle, as if made of burnt paper. Once her spirit had completely left her body, it collapsed in large, flaky ashes. The shards of ice that had been growing dropped to the ground and began melting.

"Did it work?" Pip asked.

Arleith held up the hazelnut and smiled when he saw a slight green shimmer around the surface. "I think we made it in time."

"That's great!" she clapped her hands and then immediately turned and punched Arleith in the arm. "What were you thinking? You don't make deals with faeries!"

Her punch hurt a lot more than he expected one would and a small grunt of pain came with a wince. "You heard that, then?"

"Every word," Pip hissed. "I get you there and back, only for you to mess up literally at the finish line?"

Arleith just stood, pocketing the hazelnut and looking to the Rift. "It's not a big deal, Pip."

"You're not worried about what'll happen if Frostbite says no?" Pip asked, sounding

Strawberries and Stones

confused and concerned.

"Nah," Arleith shrugged. "That'd be far worse than any kind of punishment."

Pip let her jaw go slack in awe as he started heading for the Rift. It took her a few seconds to decide to stand back up and follow him. Arleith watched her turn back, looking almost lost or forlorn as she was about to leave. He'd seen that look before, nearly twenty years ago. It was the same look his mother would give the forest whenever they had been camping and needed to return home.

Arleith put a hand on her shoulder and looked out across the meadow. "We'll come back. It'll be your adventure next time."

"Promise?" she said, still gazing out at the eternal sunset colors in the sky.

"Well, I can't see the future, so I don't know what else might come up," Arleith patted her back. "But, I'll try."

She accepted it enough to walk through the Rift with him, but she didn't turn her head back around until it was long out of sight. Arleith wasn't sure what she was thinking and couldn't help but feel bad for her. It was almost like she had been made for the Feywild when they were in there together and there were more than a few hints that she wouldn't have minded staying.
Watching her make a heavy sigh before the corners of her mouth turned back into a smile and her stride once again became a skip, he guessed the only reason she didn't decide to stay behind was because of her family. He sighed himself, drawing another parallel to his long deceased mother. It bothered him to notice how little he thought of her and was almost equally concerned that she'd only come back into his mind in the Feywild. Arleith shook his head clear again. That was a problem for a different day. They needed food and rest.

Without spending time combing the forest for the Rift and quite possibly walking in circles, once the two of them had their bearings they realized they weren't too far from home. Another day and a half at most if they stopped and camped. Neither of them wanted to hunt, despite now being in an area where it was safe to gather and collect food. They were far too exhausted.
Begrudgingly gulping down one more of Pip's berries, they began the run back to the Argentum Bastian.

They managed to cut the time down significantly and by nightfall they were beginning to see the familiar roads that led the way home. Arleith had to stop and stare at the sky. It was clear enough tonight to see some stars. After however long with a constantly orange or purple, starless sky, it was breathtaking to see them again. Even though there were only a few to pick out as the mist got thicker, he once again was brought back to a memory of his mother. She loved stargazing and would take him camping on the mountains just for a clear view of the sky. Pip followed his gaze and halted herself.

"Oh wow! I didn't think they got that beautiful!" she gasped. "Hey! Who's out there?"
The two looked at each other in confusion, Arleith speaking first in a hushed tone. "A patrol? Out here?"

There weren't usually patrols this far out beyond the borders of the city. Pip put a shushing finger to the tip of her snout and the two of them crept through the underbrush, trying to figure out how they could slip back into town. Spotting several other pairs of soldiers walking out on patrol, making it impossible to be seen. Arleith was positive they were going to face some sort of repercussions for their absence and he didn't want to chance getting caught. Pip on the other hand, let Arleith get further ahead of her before popping up.

"Oh hey! Hi!" she shouted loudly. "You know, hide and seek isn't usually played with weapons." "What are you doing?" Arleith growled a whisper at her.

"Giving you an opening," she winked before dashing off in a different direction, shouting again, "You can't just switch to tag in the middle of the game! You can't catch me anyway!"

Arleith groaned and ran his hand down his face. It had been a nice thought that she might have calmed her strangeness by having another closer friend than just her two family members, but it seemed that her weirdness was back in full force now that they were home again. Not wasting the opportunity though, he slipped back into town. As his feet touched the familiar streets, he noticed that there was a lot that had been moved since his departure. If anything, it looked like the clan was prepared to march off to battle, but the amount of carts and supplies were for a much further journey than the drow and duergar would have needed.

His attention shifted as he heard several soldiers walking down the main street. Pip was in the center of a circle of six, her hands bound behind her back and one of them guiding her with his grip on the back of her neck.

"Oh my! So rough! I don't mean to disappoint you, but I'm not into this kind of thing," she was chattering without taking a breath. "Wait, aren't you married? Oooh, you're going to be in trouble! Don't worry, I won't tell-"

Strawberries and Stones

"Shut up, Pip!" the soldier snarled and Arleith could see the muscles in his arm tighten as he shook her slightly.

"Stand down, soldier!" Arleith snapped, unable to sit by after seeing that.

All six of the patrol jumped slightly, recognizing the voice and turning to face him. The one holding his grip on Pip's neck released her and put his hand behind his back as if to hide his actions. They all saluted with dragonborn salutes while Pip used her tail to make a human salute.

"L-lieutenant! We didn't know-"

Arleith ignored them, pushing his way into the circle to Pip. He inspected the back of her neck and saw that while the skin hadn't been broken, there were marks where the claws had dug into her skin.

"What is the meaning of this? She is a superior officer and the sister of the Praetora! Where is your discipline and respect?"

"Sir," one of the female soldiers said nervously, "we've been told to bring her back alive by any means necessary. We didn't want her to escape."

"And what makes you think she'd try to escape, soldier?" Arleith glared at her with his officer intensity he saved for new recruits. "You do realize that if she wanted to, she could leave at any

time because of how much more experienced than you she is, right? I recommend thinking a little more before taking actions that are unnecessary."

"Y-yes, sir!" she stammered in return. "Um… sir? We've been ordered to do the same with you…"

Arleith took out one of his daggers and sliced the rope binding Pip's wrists. "Lead the way then, soldier."

The group of them looked nervously to each other, but seemed a bit more at ease when he re-sheathed his dagger and stood up straight with his head high and shoulders back. Waiting for them to escort them, Arleith followed without further comment in full stride with Pip by his side. Unsurprisingly, they were marched to the prison. Pip was politely asked to step into one of the cells while Arleith was given a chair to wait outside her door. Two of them departed, the rest stayed and guarded the

A Tale From the Argentum Bastian

two of them, looking more uneasy by the second.

It was only about ten minutes, but it felt so much longer. The door to the prison opened and Praetora B'lanna walked in alone. "All of you, out."

There was a crispness to her voice that made the two officers gulp visibly, but fortunately for them, no one else saw it. B'lanna waited for the door to close before she stared down Arleith and Pip, dark circles under her eyes telling them that she had lost a lot of sleep recently.

"Would either of you mind," she started calmly, but through grit teeth before raising her voice to an outright scream, "explaining where in the Nine Hells you have been? I have faeries that are angry, a war to prepare for, and my two best rangers up and disappear on me! For five months! What were you doing? Speak, now!"

Arleith felt his eyes widen in shock. Five months? It suddenly made so much more sense. The war supplies must have meant that the other dragonborn clans were in agreement, which meant they would be heading North relatively soon. It also explained why the Praetora seemed so frayed and haggard. She would be the one coordinating the logistics while the Praetor readied the army. They had also disappeared for that long without saying goodbye and while it probably didn't matter to her that he had done so, Pip would have felt like another departure like Gol'rotta's to her.

"How'd you know we were together?" Pip piped in more cheerily than appropriate.

B'lanna's eye twitched. "You both disappeared the same day and reappeared the same day. An infant could have figured it out!"

"It was my fault," Pip cut in when Arleith went to speak. "I had this sudden notion that I should explore the forest and Spire saw me leave. When I happened on the Rift to the Feywild, I really wanted to go in. Spire caught up in time and followed me. We were a little lost after that

because I really couldn't help but wander around, but we did find our way back! It was all thanks to Spire! He saved my life in there."

B'lanna ground her fangs together and turned on Arleith. "Is this true?" He gave a hesitant exhale and said, "In a manner of speaking, it's not-"
"No explanations, no addendums, yes or no," B'lanna cut him off. "Do I make myself clear?" "Yes," Arleith nodded. "It's true." It was true on the most basic of surface levels. A trick and a game faeries liked to play when trying to sneakily sway

a conversation in a direction they wanted. B'lanna wasn't stupid and she would see right through it. However, she seemed to accept it. Despite her anger at the two of them, she was still trying to protect them as best she could from punishment.

"Very well. Return to your quarters, lieutenant. Pip is to remain here for the night to receive judgment from the Council of Elders," B'lanna said calmly, but when Arleith hesitated she snapped at him, "Leave! Now!"

"Yes ma'am," he nodded and walked quickly from the sisters, glancing back before he left to see B'lanna collapse into the chair.

She sat there several minutes, breathing slowly in and out to try and calm herself before talking to Pip alone. "You left me again…And your head… What happened? Why do you have antlers now?"

"Aww, don't worry about it! I think they're amazing!" Pip squeezed through the bars so that she could sit next to her. "And I'm back now, right?"

"But what if you hadn't come back?" B'lanna was frantic, her face truly scared as she looked at her. "What if you were hurt, or lost? I can't take this anymore… I can't be alone…"

"You're never alone," Pip tried to sound comforting. "You've got Toe-biter and Digger and-"

"It's not the same, Pip," B'lanna sighed. "They're in my vicinity, but they're not close. I am trapped by my duties. I only have two people in my life who make it so that I don't feel lonely. You and Frostbite. That's all I had, and now she's gone. I should have said something. I should have done something. She would have, for me. How quickly her scales tarnished right before my eyes because I wasn't brave enough for her. She must hate me, and I don't blame her. And you… you never come by anymore… I can't remember the last time you came over to have dinner with me…"

"She doesn't hate you…" Pip whispered, but in such a way that it didn't sound like she believed it. "I'd come by more… but I don't like Toe-biter. He makes you cry and says that I cause you trouble.

So I figured it was better to stay away… no one at your house likes me anyway…"

"Pip… you are my sister… You are always welcome in my home. I don't care what the Council or the Praetor think," she hugged the smaller dragonborn. "I just want my family back. Just you, me and Frostbite, like when we were young.”

“Would that be what you want most in the world?” Pip asked, a slight upbeat in her tone. “Of course it is,” B’lanna squeezed her even tighter. “Promise you’ll never leave me again.” “Psssh!” Pip laughed. “Well I gotta leave sometimes. But, I promise, never forever.”
B’lanna sniffled, her eyes red as they had already shed all the tears they could sometime earlier in the day, “Fairy promise?”

Pip hugged her sister’s head to her chest. “All my promises are fairy promises.”

B’lanna nodded and stood, rubbing her eyes and trying to smile. “Okay. I should probably go. You’ll have to spend the night here and at least pretend you’re confined until we can bring you before the Council again.”

“Praetor Toe-biter trying to get me exiled again?” Pip asked as she shimmed through the bars again.

B’lanna glowered darkly, her tired eyes filled with fire. “If he knows what’s good for him, he’ll drop the matter by morning.”

As she departed the prison, she nearly ran into Arleith, who had been waiting by the door. B’lanna didn’t seem surprised, but did eye him as if trying to decide if he had been eavesdropping.Seeing she had calmed a bit, but still looked on the breaking point, he bowed politely and cleared his throat.

“Ma’am, I don’t like leaving the statement as it is without some clarification.”

B’lanna gave him a weary sigh and motioned for him to follow her as they walked. “The Council of Elders will always give leniency to Pip, and she knows it. Her strangeness is not her fault.
That lies with the leadership of her childhood, which most of them were at the time. While no one really knows what to do for her now, she has proven herself a loyal member of the clan in her own way. Let her take the blame for this if she wishes. It will be listed as just another time Pip was being Pip.”

“I do understand and appreciate that, ma’am,” Arleith nodded. “But a part of the story that got left out is a little more urgent. I’m sorry to bother you with it, during all of this.”

Her shoulders slumped in resignation, though she still stood as elegantly as ever. “What is it, lieutenant?”

Strawberries and Stones

"There are hags likely coming to our city," Arleith said. "We saw one, for sure, and most likely a second, but I only heard it speak. They're looking for something they think we have. I thought maybe this was related to the Fey activity you mentioned."

"That would explain why the fog has been thicker than usual," B'lanna said slowly, her eyes darting around as she put together pieces in her head. "Good memory."

"I'm sorry ma'am, but to me it feels like it's only been roughly two weeks."

B'lanna nodded her understanding and asked, "Any idea what they're searching for?"

"No clue. Something that was hidden, but was revealed. Something they want to break. That's all I know," Arleith said.

"Perhaps it's the kresh?" B'lanna mused to herself mostly.

"Why would they be after the kresh?" Arleith felt a sense of dread creeping up his neck.

"After Captain Gol'rotta's letters, I discussed an issue that has gone unnoticed with Kreshmother I'rosha and Kurzsa," she explained. "We've decided to line the entrance to the kresh with cold iron to keep the Fey out."

"Isn't that going to cause problems?" Arleith asked in disbelief.

"In your absence, this topic has already been discussed at length," B'lanna said flatly. "I am not discussing the implications further with you. Your quarters, lieutenant."

Arleith looked up and saw that they were in front of his house. Stiffly clearing his throat, he gave a saluting bow to the Praetora. "My apologies. Goodnight, Praetora."

She gave a slight bow of her head before turning back up the street to head towards her own home. Arleith stepped inside and began removing armor pieces so that he could lay down in his bed. Dust kicked up as different pieces hit the table to await treatment when he woke. The weapons and larger pieces off, he had to pause when he removed his bracers. On his right wrist was a tattoo of a thorn covered vine that was wrapped around four times, crossing on the inside of his wrist and the outside. He wasn't sure what it meant or why it was put there, but it was a reminder that he had agreed to be punished for stealing the iolite if Gol'rotta refused him.

A Tale From the Argentum Bastian

He laid down on the bed with an exhausted groan, letting his aching muscles finally relax after days of running. There wasn't much else to do now, besides wait for whatever happened next. He'd care for his armor and weapons in the morning and then get started shaping and polishing the iolite to turn it into a proper Tlhogh Stone. With that in mind, he drifted off into a restful sleep, grateful to be back home.

Things were fairly quiet for the next few weeks. As his official station was still in the reserves for the time being, Arleith was not called upon to help load wagons or maintain weapons. He wasn't even asked to help train cadets that would be old enough for their five year compulsory service. He used the time to work on shaping the iolite, taking the most traditional methods to chip away and smooth out edges. Classically, dragonborn did so with nothing but their claws and scales and Arleith found the process soothing to the mind. It was similar to oiling his armor and weapons. A focused task that didn't leave much time to dwell on what was around him. It was a lot slower than the chisels and tumblers most used now, but he was proud of his work.

"Hey, Spire!" Pip cheerfully popped in one day. The first time since their adventure. "I have an errand I need to run. Wanna come with?"

"Sure," he shrugged, putting down the rag he'd been using to wipe the dust from the gem. "What do you need to get done?"

Pip eyed the stone as he set it down and smiled at him. "You know what, you're busy. I should probably just take care of it myself anyway."

"You sure? I don't mind taking a break," Arleith offered.

"No, no!" Pip insisted. "Besides, it's probably going to involve lots of girl talk and general lady stuff that you probably don't want to hear."

"If you're sure," Arleith shrugged again, sitting down and going back to his work. "Let me know if you change your mind."

She left, chipper as usual for her and he didn't think much of it. The following day, he was finishing the final polish on the iolite and sat back to admire his handiwork. Its shape was definitely more teardrop than candle flame, but the surface was perfectly even and smooth, tapering to a fine point that could have been used as a spear head. What made it work as he intended though, was the way it gathered and refracted light. Due to the shape and the way he had polished it, the gem seemed to glow in the more bulbous end, looking like a lavender flame with an almost white hot core.

Strawberries and Stones

There was a pounding rap on the door that stopped him from looking at it too long. "One minute."

The door slammed open, splintering where the latch had once been and cracking almost completely in half. Praetora B'lanna stormed into his house, her voice furious and a little crazed. "Where is she?"

Arleith stopped in confusion, not sure why she was doing this or who she was talking about. "I don't-"

As he spoke, she muttered something under her breath and made a quick gesture with her arms before bolting into the room, cutting him off with a grip to his throat. She lifted him off the ground with ease, only using one arm as she repeated herself. "Where is she?"

Arleith could see the magic she had used on herself, radiating off her body like a listing red steam as she glared at him, her fury clear in her eyes. From his elevated position, he could see one of her Praetorian Guards, the same one he recognized, from when she had asked him to meet in her office. There was a drake there as well, with the same patterns in its scales, but much, much larger, as if she were constantly being fed.

Arleith knew that whatever had the Praetora in this state, it wasn't his doing, so he stared right back at her, managing to speak around her grip. "You done?"

"You'll know when I'm done," she snarled back.

"I can't help you until I know what's going on," Arleith said defiantly.

With a growl and a huff, she roughly brought him back down on his feet. She stumbled herself a little, as if dizzy, making both the Guard and Arleith rush to her side. They were halted by a held up hand.

"It's fine, I'm fine," but the anger rising in her voice sounded anything but what she insisted. "Everything is fine!"

"Can I help you with your initial problem then?" Arleith asked a little more dryly than he intended. While he didn't appreciate the intrusion, he didn't want to anger her more.

"Pip is gone. She was here yesterday."

A Tale From the Argentum Bastian

"Worried about a repeat from me?" Arleith asked as he readjusted his tunic.

"I don't know what to think anymore," B'lanna snapped as she paced back and forth. "But I woke up this morning with this stuck to my forehead with jam!"

She thrust a piece of parchment in his face and he had to do his best not to laugh, managing to contain it into a tiny snort that resonated in his snout.

Be back soon, Promise!

At the bottom, instead of a signature, was a drawing of a tiny strawberry. Arleith cleared his throat and unclenched his face from containing his laughter and spoke. "I swear to you, I have no idea what this is about. All she mentioned was an errand yesterday."

B'lanna continued pacing, chewing on one of her claws until she noticed the glint of the gem on the table. She stopped and slowly picked it up, carefully examining it. "It was your idea, wasn't it? This is where you two went."

Arleith nodded. "Yeah. I wanted to clear that up but you said everything would be fine."

She was quiet a long time, turning it over in her hand and looking at it from every possible angle. Her anger seemed to melt away and was replaced with another extreme in emotion. Her eyes started to look wet, like she might cry, but it seemed like she was far more practiced keeping it in. She looked up and gracefully walked back towards him.

"Consider yourself under house arrest until further notice," she said sternly, but at the same time, carefully placed the stone into his hand. "Perhaps we can discuss where you see your future in the clan after the arrival of your captain and she decides what to do with you. I'm sending some soldiers to retrieve her, now that we have our course of action set for Frostbane."

Arleith wasn't entirely sure what she meant, but he got the impression she saw what she was doing as a favor. "Yes, ma'am."

B'lanna bowed her head slightly before taking her departure, addressing the drake in the entryway. "Come, Draga! Let's see if we can get you a fish snack at the docks!"

Arleith saw the Praetorian Guard set his jaw and his nostrils flare in a vent of silent frustration, lifting his head to the sky. He turned and nodded to Arleith before following the Praetora. He caught up quickly, remaining silent beside her as she walked, scratching the drake's head at the same time.

"I saw that, Sarik," she said casually to her bodyguard before three others broke away from Arleith's house and joined them. "Did you want to say something?"

"Nothing I haven't said before, ma'am," he grumbled.

"Draga is a good girl. She deserves a treat. Don't you, girl?" B'lanna cooed at the drake, which looked up at her and frantically started wiggling at the praise. "Yes, you do!"

Sarik grumbled again, but said nothing as the other three fell in line around her. They escorted her to a coach that was pulled by a pair of giant rams. Sarik entered with her while the other

three piled on top and with the driver. During the ride, B'lanna continued petting Draga, but her mind was elsewhere. Why couldn't her family just stay in one place? Every time she had one of them closer, the other seemed further away. Absently, one hand rested on her stomach as she nervously thought about bringing them all together again. The three of them had a lot to talk about and she personally felt like she had bridges to repair. Whether or not she was successful, she wouldn't be alone anymore at least.

If anything, Pip did promise she would be back. Since they were children, Pip was very particular about promises, stating that faeries only made promises they could keep. A Fairy Promise to the siblings had meant that it was a promise they would keep at any cost. She was more worried about Gol'rotta. Her cousin was not one who enjoyed being told what to do. She was stubborn to the point of defiance if it was something she absolutely did not want to do.
B'lanna's biggest fear was that she would be seen as forcing her cousin to return, and given the circumstances, she had always been afraid to allow herself to consider that she did not want to return. The fact that she needed to stand before the Praetors and Praetoras from all the clans and tell them what she had witnessed while away was more of a convenient excuse for B'lanna to coax Gol'rotta back.

Without realizing it, the coach ride had passed and when she opened the door, she was greeted by the smell of sea air and freshly caught fish. The three guards on the outside jumped down and fell in around her again, while Sarik followed behind with Draga. The human port town seemed so filthy to her, compared to the Argentum Bastian. The beach was nothing but grey shale, covered in the droppings of sea birds and the cobblestone streets were so caked in mud that it almost felt like an effort in futility to stay on the paths. The sky was equally dreary and probably cold, judging by how bundled up the fishermen were in wool coats. She raised the hem of her dress with a single hand, gracefully striding toward the one building that seemed somewhat maintained. Cleaned and lacquered far more than the sea swollen shacks that lined the streets were the dock offices. She entered and approached a clean cut sailor behind a desk.

"Can I help you?" he asked as B'lanna looked for a place to sit.

"I am Praetora B'lanna. I had sent ahead for a charter to Westfall for a messenger," she stated.

"Unless I'm mistaken, I believe we fulfilled that request yesterday," he checked his charter logs. "Yes, here it is. One messenger for passage to Westfall, return charter with an unspecified number of return guests."

B'lanna blinked incredulously at him. "What?"

"Yeah, a dragonborn came through yesterday. Smallest one I've ever seen actually. Said she was selected personally for the job a few weeks ago. Seemed very proud of it. Flashed an officer's insignia and everything."

B'lanna's eye twitched and she started breathing through her nose in a way that quickly escalated to nearly hyperventilating. Sarik offered her a hand to hold so that she could steady herself as she started getting dizzy. Wordlessly, she nodded to the sailor and turned to leave, tightly gripping his hand. The Praetorian Guards walked her back to the coach, one holding up the hem of B'lanna's dress. Sarik helped her in while the others jumped back on top to get ready for departure. When B'lanna was seated, Sarik waited outside for a moment, closing the door and turning his back to it, ready to send anyone away that approached. With force if necessary. Alone inside, the Praetora's still escalated breathing stilled for a moment as she drew in a deep breath. Grabbing a cushion from the seat, she buried her face into it and screamed.

Strawberries and Stones

****

Five days at sea and Pip had barely left the bow of the ship, excitedly feeling the swell of the waves and rolling her body with them as the ship sailed East. The crew kept shooting her odd looks as they passed her while doing their duties. They had dealt with dragonborn a lot in the last five months, but they had all been far more… stoic.

Pip didn't care. It was actually far more entertaining to see a different species be weirded out by her. Human faces had so many expressions compared to dragonborn. Her favorite was the way they scrunched up their faces when in pain. No dragonborn, not even her, did much more than bare their fangs when they felt pain. While she wanted to find more pins and tacks to put in prime sitting places, she was far more excited when she saw land on the horizon. While they were still a few days away, she was assured it was the sheer cliff wall that made the coastal side of Westfall.

She smiled and whispered to herself as it drew nearer. "See you soon, Frostbite!"

A Tale From the Argentum Bastian

⟨decorative script line⟩

⟨decorative script⟩ (The Gorgon)

As many mothers often did in the Argentum Bastian, there were several leaning on the fenced in play area for the children of the clan. Kresh Mother I'rosha, old and weathered as she was, didn't miss a beat as she watched them play. Currently one of the largest and most powerful warriors in the clan, the mother that stood out the most was Gol'thaga. The powerful, scaled and clawed hands of the silver dragonborn gripped the wood in front of her, drawing a creak from the crushed fibers. No one was supposed to play favorites in the clan, so parents weren't allowed to know which child was theirs after they hatched until they were old enough to be brought home. It was a clan rule and tradition, but the mothers all knew. The undertones of their skin beneath their scales matched the color of their baby's egg. Such a subtle thing was easy to miss, but it was a secret many mothers passed down to each other.

Gol'thaga was no different. She watched her daughter running and playing with the child that was born to her brother and his mate. Her child was large, naturally strong like herself and her father. She couldn't help but watch with pride as one of the older boys failed to knock her over with a tackle. Only a little longer. Her tenth birthday was still a few weeks away, but then she could finally come home.

"Keep staring that hard and they'll know you know," a mellow, bass voice startled her and caused her to whip around.

Face to face with her husband, Gol'thaga punched him in the shoulder. "Quit sneaking up on me like that!"

He smirked, but said nothing, leaning on the fence to look at the playing children as well. Rotta'ghan was not much of a talker, but like his mate, he was tall and strong, even by the standards of the clan. Gol'thaga relaxed and leaned next to him again, though not gripping the fence this time. Her mate took a cigar from a small box tucked into a pouch at his waist, digging out a lighter a gnome had made for him as a thank you. Lighting it, he took a long drag, drawing a scowl from Gol'thaga.

"I told you to quit," she grumbled as he let out a plume of smoke from his nostrils.

"I've got some time to enjoy what's left," Rotta'ghan said dismissively.

Gol'thaga growled at him but her tone was soft as she looked back at the kresh. "You didn't forget we'll have all three, right?"

The cigar stopped moving in his mouth as he considered this fact. Families were small in Clan Sivak, with most parents only having one child. Gol'thaga was unusual for having a sibling, but it was a fact that didn't last long into adulthood. Her brother had died fighting off a troupe of wendigos shortly after his mate had announced that she was having a second egg. It usually made Rotta'ghan wonder if they too would have a second child and start a family tradition, but his thoughts didn't stray in that direction this time. Gol'thaga's sister in law had died as well recently, leaving her as the closest family relative the two children would have. Gol'thaga had agreed to take the children in when the time came without hesitation. A very full house.

Gol'thaga smiled as she watched him take another long drag before grinding out the embers and tucking it back away. They watched a little longer together, with the mother resting her head on her husband's shoulder briefly before they left to continue getting their home ready.

Over the next few days, Gol'thaga fussed about every aspect of their spartan home. While there wasn't much to do, she was having a hard time sitting still as the day drew nearer. Rotta'ghan did his best to keep her calm, which usually only took a hand on her shoulder, but he knew seeing her daughter brought home was something she'd been looking forward to since the day the egg was laid.

Their busy work was interrupted by one of the generals of their army stopping by. Trei'zdek was the general that their chain of command reached up toward. He was someone they both respected and were respected by in turn. The two of them stood at attention as soon as they saw him and saluted. He did the same before bowing in front of them.

"Well met, you two," the general said. "I hope you're doing well."

"Yes, sir," Gol'thaga spoke as if it were her drill instructor while her husband nodded. "If I may ask, sir, why are you here?"

"I apologize," the general bowed again. "I know you're on leave to receive your child-"

"And my niece," Gol'thaga added, and Rotta'ghan could feel her defiance ready to

A Tale From the Argentum Bastian

resurface as they both sensed incoming orders.

"I know," the general grimaced as he prepared to continue, "but we've lost contact with a mine scouting detail. I'm gathering a task force for a search and rescue and I need the best. We can't afford to lose any income to the clan. I'd only ask for one of you, but this is dire or I wouldn't ask at all."

"I'll go," Rotta'ghan spoke first, catching his wife off guard. Seeing the look in her eyes, he decided to explain himself this time. "The girls are coming. You're not going to miss it."

"You're not either," she growled, the tone he knew was nerves and not anger. "How long?"

"They went missing near Crossroad Pass. Not far, but be prepared for anything. I anticipate four days at most," Trei'zdek stated. "The team will be meeting this afternoon."

Crossroad Pass was in the Underdark, but not deep. It was a fairly close, barely more than a day's march. The Sivak had some smaller gem mines nearby. The area had high traffic of several groups, being the Sivak, drow, duergar and the deep gnomes, so it was usually a neutral area so as to not start problems that pulled in other factions. It was odd for a scouting crew to go missing, but not unheard of.

"I'll go," Gol'thaga insisted, receiving a scowl from her husband. "I'm driving you crazy and I need something to do. This waiting is killing me, so something to focus on will do me good."

Rotta'ghan didn't look convinced and his steely gaze bore into her. Feeling uncomfortable watching the debate, Trei'zdek cleared his throat to interject, only to draw their glares onto himself. "Report to the barracks once you've decided, please."

As he hastened away, the two looked back to each other, but Gol'thaga softened her expression. "I need to do something. I won't be long, I just need to occupy myself before I turn you insane. You know I'll be fine."

"You always are," Rotta'ghan agreed. "But what if this takes a while? I'm not going to the Kresh without you."

"Then I'll hurry back," Gol'thaga hugged her mate reassuringly. "I won't make them wait."

Gorgon and Granite

With a grumble, Rotta'ghan nodded. The two embraced before she went to gather her things. Gol'thaga always traveled light. Changing into her uniform, she put on the harness she used to carry her weapons. She didn't need armor, but her Tlogh Stone, her symbol of her marriage, was set into the center of the harness. For her, that was all the protection she needed. Grabbing her trusty maul, she inspected her ancestral weapon. Taking a moment to grin at all of the names engraved into the haft, her family lineage, all great warriors.

She asked her ancestors to watch over her family while she was away before marching to the barracks.

There was little noise coming from within as she opened the door. General Trei'zdek was there with half a dozen soldiers. Gol'thaga recognized them all by reputation. Scarred, focused, veterans. The general hadn't been exaggerating when he said he needed the best. They stood and saluted, a closed fist over their chest, as she approached.

"This it?" she asked. "We're all?"

"All that we can spare at the moment," Trei'zdek nodded. "We're stretched thin right now with the majority of the army at both the drow front and the duergar. Everyone here was either on leave or Reprieve."

Several of the task force looked at each other. Gol'thaga was known for her impatience that bordered on insubordination, but the fact the general allowed it was something they hadn't expected. Regardless, the look was one of amused respect and they let them continue.

"As the only one with rank, I'm putting you in charge," Trei'zdek added. "Find our kin and bring them home."

"Yes, sir!" the room responded in unison.

There was little need for further talk. They all knew where they were supposed to start and there was little else to go on beyond that. The small unit headed towards the mountains, each grabbing a pack of rations on their way out. Gol'thaga appreciated that it didn't really matter who was there. Everyone was a career soldier, everyone knew their place and what to do. As they got outside the village, her scout, one of the two other females of the expedition, hustled up to speak with her.

"Never thought I'd get to work alongside the great Gorgon," she nervously chuckled.

A Tale From the Argentum Bastian

"Nor I you, Whiptail," Gol'thaga smirked as she acknowledged her.

She paused a moment, stunned for a second before trotting back up to her side. "I never would have guessed you'd know the name of a ranger."

"We all fight," Gol'thaga snorted, sending a plume of frost from her snout. "So long as it's for the clan, I respect all warriors."

The younger warrior looked away, abashed. Gol'thaga could guess that she might have been given Reprieve by the way she carried herself. She fidgeted and kept looking around as if being followed. A long, deep scar ran down the side of her face and through an eye that was covered by an eyepatch. Paranoid and sharp hearing. It would work in their favor in the Underdark, but with her maternal side coming out she wanted nothing more than to see to it she made it back safely. She was so young. Reprieve was coming earlier and earlier it seemed as their endless battles raged beneath the Evergloom Peaks.

There was little chatter beyond that once they started closing in on the base of the mountain. Whiptail took point as the lead scout, her abnormally thin tail flicking nervously at any sound out of the ordinary. Gol'thaga looked at the rest to size them up and figure out their strengths.

An exceptionally burly, but short dragonborn named Grimjaw stood nearby. Across his back was a massive shield that would have taken some members of the clan two hands to wield. He could usually wedge himself into a tunnel and stop anything from making it past him. About the same age as her, Gol'thaga knew he was on leave for grieving his wife's passing. To her it looked like he was more ready to kill than to cry.

Not far was the only other one on Reprieve and one of the few she didn't know the Kresh Name of. Ulna'thaan had once been a captain too, but a wound to her throat had taken away her ability to breathe frost or speak above a whisper. Still a strong fighter, but her pride would not see her demoted because of disability.

The other three, Razortooth, Pit and Ivy, were all part of her unit on leave as well. Since she, their commanding officer, was on leave it had turned into a bit of a vacation for them as well. Most of her unit had been temporarily reassigned, but some were rotated in as watches for the village. They were all dependable, if a little restless, but that was why she had requested them in the first place. For her, it was a relief that they were there.

As they approached the entrance to the cave systems they knew, Gol'thaga barked a few orders to her crew. "Grim, Razor, I want you two guarding the rear. Captain, Ivy and Pit, center for support and protecting supplies. I'll take point with Whiptail from here."

"Yes, ma'am!" they shouted in unison, easily falling in line without breaking their pace as they entered the caverns.

Gol'thaga let Whiptail go a few paces ahead of her as they followed the paths the clan had widened. The young girl seemed more focused and at ease in the tunnels. She slipped down side paths quickly before motioning the patrol onward. It would have surprised Gol'thaga if their enemies had come this close to their territory, or if any monsters had managed to get that close to the surface. It was always a possibility though, so no chances were taken.

They marched the entire day, not even stopping to set up camp to eat. Passing out rations, they kept on the move as Gol'thaga and Whiptail kept changing places to give each other rest. Time didn't really matter when you couldn't see the difference between night and day. Eventually they all did get tired, but it became a game to see who could hold out the longest. It lasted for a long while until Pit was finally the one to cave.

"We ever gonna stop to eat, Gorgon?" he caught up to her enough to whisper.

Gol'thaga smirked and asked loudly and clearly, "Are you willing to suffer the consequences for being the one to ask to make camp, soldier?"

Pit groaned and let out an exasperated, "Yeah…"

"You heard him!" Gol'thaga laughed. "Take a breather everyone. We move again in one hour."

They all dropped their packs gratefully and took a seat on the sloping floor. Pit begrudgingly began preparing the rations while everyone else got as comfortable as the tunnels would allow. Gol'thaga used her pack to lay out a map and go over the paths. Based on the number of offshoots and passages they had already gone by, it would only be another two hours before they reached the mine. They had made good time so far. While looking, Ulna'thaan sat next to her and voiced a concern she'd had in the back of her mind as well.

"Are we worried we haven't seen any trace of them yet?" her rasping whisper only reached Gol'thaga.

A Tale From the Argentum Bastian

"Hard to say," she said, studying the map. "Maybe they're in trouble, maybe they hit a good haul."

"They didn't send word though," the older dragonborn said skeptically.

"Doesn't matter. We either find them or find out what happened to them," Gol'thaga eyed her carefully. "You have any problems with the way I run things, Captain?"

Ulna'thaan shook her head, ignoring the questioning jab. "It's not my style, but I know even the best plans can go to hell in an instant. Just getting your thoughts, ma'am."

"It's appreciated," Gol'thaga clasped her shoulder. "Get some rest, grab a bite before Pit eats it all. It'll be fine"

"I request you don't call me 'Captain' though. That's long behind me now."

Gol'thaga gave her a wry smile. "We don't just forget this stuff. You earned your rank. Just because you can't shout, it won't take any of that away, Ulna'thaan."

The older dragonborn smiled and nodded her appreciation before rejoining the others while the captain folded her map and put it away with a sigh. She didn't like the situation either, but she didn't want to show it in front of the crew. It was too quiet for the Underdark. Something was wrong, but with hundreds of things it could be and the fact that each of them had different ways to be dealt with, it was impossible to prepare.

Her concerns were interrupted by the bass rumble of Grimjaw's voice. "You planning on eating all of that?"

Looking up, Gol'thaga saw Pit defensively holding a cured rabbit. "Hey, I put this in my personal pack from home!"

"Along with the parcel of raspberries and the smoked boar bacon and the biscuits," Razortooth smirked. "Amongst other things."

"Where does he even put it all?" Ulna'thaan chuckled. "I've never seen anyone eat that much."

"That's why Kresh Mama called him Pit," Ivy slung an arm around her friend. "Because feeding him is like throwing food into a bottomless hole."

Gorgon and Granite

"And yet he's still not even close to as tall as Gorgon," Whiptail nodded towards Gol'thaga.

"Alright, leave the poor maw alone," Gol'thaga laughed. "Ivy, play something for us. Girl's voice is like magic."

Ivy smiled and took a pan flute from a satchel at her hip. Without warming up, she went into a soothing melody. It didn't take long for the rest of the crew to pick up on the song and start humming and tapping along with her. It was a lullaby that the fairies often sang whenever the Argentum Bastion could actually see the moon through the mist that blanketed the valley. As they listened to the soft tune, the small strike force felt relaxed and invigorated as they finished their break and put their gear back on. The tension was eased quite a bit too, for most of the younger members of the team. It made their pace quicker for the final stretch, practically jogging the rest of the way.

As they got closer to the entrance, Whiptail held up a fist and put her one good eye near the ground. When Gol'thaga caught up, the smaller female whispered, "Tripwire."

Gol'thaga immediately signaled the rest to halt and squatted next to her scout. "Can you disarm it?"

She shook her head. "Silver thread. Magical in nature. I could probably dispel it, but-"

"Save it for now," Gol'thaga growled as she scanned the darkness for movement. "As long as we know where it is. I want you all fresh."

Whiptail nodded and took out a piece of chalk. Careful to be quiet, she marked the level of the thread while Gol'thaga silently signaled the rest of the crew. Drow nearby. Drawing weapons and pulling shields if they had them, Gol'thaga nodded her approval before stepping over the line Whiptail had marked. Stealth wasn't something most Sivak were well practiced in, so only a couple of them darted behind cover while the rest walked quietly and alert. Gol'thaga was careful around the support beams holding up the high ceiling of the mine. The drow had several tricks that made it easy for them to hide anywhere.

Gol'thaga nodded to Ivy. The young cadet took out a fiddle and hummed a few chords in a low tone before gliding the bow across the strings. It didn't make any sound that the rescue party could hear, but the frequency resonated in a way that the bardess could understand. Scanning the area and listening, she eventually turned back to the captain and shook her head, letting the leader know she didn't detect anything using her magical abilities. The crew still didn't take any chances, inching along until they spotted the first person.

Motioning for them to set a perimeter, Gol'thaga hurried over to the limp form, followed closely by Ivy. After a check of the surroundings, they spotted the rest of the miners and guards. All were accounted for, but unconscious. The rest of the squad came in, with Grimjaw and Razortooth watching their backs while they tended to the mining team. It didn't take long for them to find small bolts from drow hand crossbows piercing through a few of them, others had puncture wounds where they likely ripped the projectiles from their flesh. Gol'thaga could feel the residue of the sleep toxins drow used on her claws as she pulled them free.

Using smelling salts, the workers began to stir. Gol'thaga did her best to keep from getting impatient, waiting for them to be ready to move. The very idea suddenly shook her. She was going to need patience very soon. A lot of it. Her muscles slackened in the darkness as she thought about her daughter. Would they get along? What would they do together? Would she want to be held? Was she too old to be held?

Her thoughts were loud enough that it took Ivy grabbing her shoulder and gently shaking Gol'thaga out of her imagination. "Captain? What's wrong?"

Her soldier's whisper was quiet enough for the others to not have heard but was enough for Gol'thaga to regain her focus. Her muscles rippled and flexed as she gripped her maul again. "It's fine. I'm fine. Let's get them up and get the hell out of here."

She could tell Ulna'thaan was having similar apprehensions as they slowly got the miners to their feet. It was too easy. The entrance had been set with an alarm tripwire and their people had only been knocked out. Gol'thaga watched carefully as her team went to the last of the people they had been sent to rescue. Gradually as they all came to, the foreman looked to have a thick mass of sticky thread attached to his back as Pit propped him up. There was no time to call out before they went taut as they stopped the foreman from getting up. A thin hood of spider webbing pulled upward like a lid on a slowly opening jar before it burst open. A massive spider unfurled from the hidden burrow beneath, its numerous long legs wrapping around the two dragonborn with fangs spread toward them.

Gol'thaga was prepared though. Just as the creature came free, she was halfway across the room and readying a massive swing. She didn't hit the spider, however. As she suspected, a dark figure almost completely lost in the darkness rose up with the spider. Mounted on its back was a drow, scanning the room and getting their bearings to aim a one handed crossbow at one of the rescue team. As the reflective, red eyes picked out a target, the heavy maul smashed into the dark elf's ribcage, lifting them out of the saddle as the blow flung the already dead body across the room. Gol'thaga used the momentum to bull her shoulder into the spider, knocking it away from the foreman and her younger squadmate.

The maul came up over her head and straight down, easily splitting the exoskeleton as she pulverized its head.

"If you can feel your legs, you better use them!" Gol'thaga roared. "It's time to go!"

The miners jolted upright at the call, while those that couldn't were helped up or carried by others. Other trapdoor spiders the size of wagons burst from their own holes, most bearing a drow rider. There was movement shifting further down the mine as a wave of warriors slunk from the shadows. The dragonborn captain rushed in, her size occupying enough of the tunnel to make it difficult to pass without getting their skulls bashed in.

While most of her team came to help, Gol'thaga shouted her orders. "Ulna'thaan, you get the workers out! You're in charge of them until I catch up! Grimjaw, you're with them! Cover the rear! I better not see a damn scratch more on them than they've already got! Ivy, between the two groups, support whoever needs it! The rest of you, with me!"

The drow broke like a wave against the rocks. None of the three at the front moved as the dark elves crashed into them. A few manage to slip by, only to be picked off by Whiptail with her bow. Pit and Razortooth shifted their stances bracing themselves and their shields against the sheer mass of dark elves. Gol'thaga, on the other hand, caught several in the throat with the haft of her weapon. The line before her staggered back, giving her plenty of room to make sweeping swings. The brutal power behind the dragonborn broke through them with ease, her heart pumping in battle lust as she began pressing forward.

Drow were fast, but not powerful by the standards of the Sivak. Their bladework was something like a dance. Elegant, beautiful, typically deadly. Many failed to account for how tough Gol'thaga's hide was though, with most of the strikes that managed to land on her barely making a scrape or completely bouncing off. Even if they managed to break her skin, the captain's muscles were like coiled steel, unyielding to the thin blades of the dark elves.

"Captain! Wall crawlers!" Whiptail called from behind her, barely registering with

A Tale From the Argentum Bastian

the much larger dragonborn.

With a low growl, Gol'thaga gave a quick glance upwards, seeing a full cavalry of drow riding spiders across the high ceilings and walls of the mine. Within minutes they'd either be surrounded or the miners would be under attack again, with only two of the rescue team close enough to protect them.

"Fall back!" Gol'thaga bellowed. "Whiptail! Ivy! I don't want them getting any closer to the other group!"

Without looking to see if her orders were being carried out, she planted her feet. Inhaling deeply, a roar akin to their dragon ancestors rang through the caverns. The fear on the elven faces was plain to see, even in the dark. With a grin, she rushed them again. Several began to flee and those that didn't were easily swept to the side by a heavy blow from Gol'thaga's maul. Smashing legs off of spiders and splitting armor with the sheer impact of her weapon, she was in her element.

Razortooth and Pit stayed a few paces back, finishing off anything that happened to survive the onslaught. It was wiser than limiting her range of motion by being shoulder to shoulder. The two were getting worried about how far apart they were from the rest of the group, but the lines were thinning and it seemed like most of the spiders were already dead. Gol'thaga knew it wasn't the end though. All of the warriors had been men. Nothing but fodder in the matriarchal society. The real fight was still coming.

As the sound of cracking whips eventually cut through the din of battle, those that had fled in terror from the relentless captain were being turned back around. Yellow liquid began to flow from behind them and pool just before Gol'thaga. It bubbled up, forming into a shape that looked like an ever melting candle. A singular eye shifted into position, level with the dragonborn's. The putrid creature reeked of demonic energy and it only took a moment for the captain to know what to do.

"Yochlol," Gol'thaga shouted.

She turned and ran as hard as she could, getting to the two younger males under her command. Grabbing both of them by the collar, she pushed them to dash away faster than they ever had before. While Gol'thaga didn't know exactly what it was, be it ooze or demon, if there was one there it meant that there was a priestess nearby to command it. It kept extending pseudopods, morphing after itself rapidly and extending again to remain just on their tails. Nearing the mine entrance, the captain shoved her two younger soldiers ahead of her. She whirled around with her maul at the ready just in time to see it spreading itself wide to engulf her.

Gorgon and Granite

There was a rumble and the scrape of metal on rock that rushed up. Grimjaw barreled into the creature, the vast size of his shield before him pushing the yochlol back with ease. Planting his feet and digging his claws into the very stone beneath him, the broad but squat dragonborn freed one hand to draw a spear and jab it into the yellow demon.

Gol'thaga rushed to his side, slamming her weapon into it as well.

"I told you to guard the miners!"

"Yup!" his normally mellow, bass voice filled with glee. "Then we heard there were demons."

Gol'thaga had to stifle a laugh as the two pushed back against the monster. The rest of their small crew quickly fell in line. Razortooth and Pit flanked Grimjaw and the captain, blocking the long tendrils that tried to lash around the enormous shield. Hacking and separating them slowed the creature down as they had to slowly crawl back to reform with the main body. Ulna'thaan threw javelins at the eye whenever it tried to bubble up over the shield for better view while Whiptail clung to the ceiling from a stalactite using her namesake and clawed feet to steady herself as she shot her bow into the ranks of backup the drow were sending. Ivy's voice cut through the noise of battle with ease, invigorating the small crew as they began to get weary.

No matter how much they did to it though, it didn't seem to be enough. It was hard to tell if their weapons were having any impact at all. Gol'thaga grit her teeth angrily as she looked at the younger members and knew they'd be overrun as soon as the drow forces closed in.

"Fall back! Everyone with shields, get to the miners! Everyone without, lead the way home! Ulna'thaan, it's your show from here! Go! NOW!"

Grimjaw and Ulna'thaan looked at her with worry deep in their faces. They nodded though, with the eldest member calling orders as best she could. The one dragon phalanx dropped his spear and braced again, making sure everyone else was clear before he moved. The younger members hesitated and lingered long enough until they got a stern glare from Gol'thaga. They broke away wordlessly, steeling their expressions before facing the wounded miners.

"Sure you're gonna be okay?" Grimjaw asked when it was just the two of them.

Gol'thaga smirked as she rotated the maul in her grip, a faint, mint green glow coming from the head of the weapon as she did so. "I live for this shit."

The two looked to each other, acknowledging Gol'thaga was ready. Grimjaw broke away, dashing a few feet before turning to walk backwards, keeping an eye on the captain while guarding the rear of the retreating Sivak. Gol'thaga was upon the creature before he had gotten clear of the yellow glop that made its body. Bringing the maul heavily into the center of its mass, the light exploded from the weapon upon impact with radiant energy. A hissing wail echoed through the mine as the yochlol recoiled, shrinking back into itself.

Gol'thaga didn't stop. As though powered by the earth itself, she pushed forward with a surge of strikes. The shrieks from an unseen mouth from the demon grew louder as it kept trying to pull away, only for the captain to close the gap again. She couldn't help but wonder if it would have felt the same as taking a hammer to pudding as it squelched with each impact, sending streaks of bright yellow flying in every direction. This time it failed to reform. It kept retreating as larger and larger drips fell from it until it seemed to melt into the floor. Only when the ichor began to curdle and turn black before evaporating was Gol'thaga satisfied that it was dead.

Her victory was shortened by a condescending clap. She only turned her eyes upward, leaving her in a menacing scowl as she looked upon a drow priestess riding atop a spider nearly the size of her hutch she shared with her husband. The dark, ebony skin was wrapped in silk spun in a web pattern under dark metal plates of armor. Floor length, silvery hair was streaked with red and purple dyes, tied back out of a pair of cruel, gleaming red eyes.

"Quite a performance," she mused in a wispy tone. "But, you are outnumbered. You can't keep it up forever. It's a shame your leaders didn't send more."

"I'm more than you can handle," Gol'thaga smirked through a growl.

Her charcoal colored lips curled in an amused smile. "Are you sure?"

She dismounted from the spider, gracefully gliding before the dragonborn. With a saber in one hand and a cat-o'-nine-tails in the other, the drow nodded to Gol'thaga before taking a fighter's stance. Gol'thaga knew she would have something up her sleeve. The drow were never ones to engage in a fair fight. She glanced around the room, analyzing the situation. She was back in the main part of the mine. The most open part of the tunnel with what looked like an army of well equipped women behind their priestess. She'd have to end things quickly if she wanted to survive.

They ran at each other at such speeds it was impossible to tell who moved first.

Gorgon and Granite

Gol'thaga narrowly avoided a lash from the whip as it cracked in the air inches from her face. She used the momentum of her body shifting out of the way to come in with an upward swing for the drow's chin. The saber caught the blow, parrying the maul away before arcing over her head and chopping down towards Gol'thaga's shoulder.

The dragonborn let the weight of her maul drop down by slackening her grip, allowing her to pivot the other end to come up and block the blade. In the split second the saber was locked in place, Gol'thaga stepped forward with a solid punch directly to the drow's jaw. She staggered backwards but as the dragonborn raised the maul over her head with both claws a flash of movement caused her to make an improvised swing to the side instead. One of the assassins accompanying the priestess had cut around and was about to strike. The maul easily shattered the bones in their shoulder and collar, dropping them to one knee. Gol'thaga grabbed the drow by the face and smashed her head into the stone wall, feeling the skull crack in her palm.

Turning back to her main quarry, the priestess had already regained her footing and was lashing the whip in her direction again. Catching it with the haft of her maul, the nine ends wrapped around it tightly and went taut. Easily overpowering the lithe elf, Gol'thaga yanked her towards herself, ready to swing her weapon over her head and into the side of the priestess' head. This time she was blocked by another warrior, crossing two blades to hold the maul in place while several others rushed her. Gol'thaga shoved the one stopping her back before inhaling deeply. She opened her mouth wide, the exhale bringing out a blast of her frost breath. They tried to cover their faces, but it did little as their flesh in the exposed path became flash frozen. Limbs and heads shattered in a spray of ice with a clean swing of her maul before turning back to their leader.

Once again she had composed herself and waited to strike while Gol'thaga was distracted. The tip of the saber was thrust forward, close enough to gouge part of her harness as she side-stepped out of the way. The priestess shifted and slashed upward for Gol'thaga's throat, making her step back again, only for the whip to crack again. The captain raised her arm, unable to get her weapon up in time to intercept, allowing all nine ends of the whip to wrap around her forearm. She grimaced as the hooked barbs dug into her flesh. Sections of her arm started to go numb and Gol'thaga knew they had to be poisoned. The wounds were barely scratches to her tough hide, meaning they hadn't penetrated enough to deliver anything lethal.

Baring her fangs, Gol'thaga grabbed the cat-o'-nine-tails and pulled, raising her maul with the other hand. The only way the priestess was going to be free of this strike would be to let go. She dropped the whip and caught the maul with her saber, forced to use her now free hand to push against the flat of the blade. The dragonborn shook the whip free and gripped the haft of her own weapon with both hands, forcing the drow to her knees.

With the priestess clearly in a vulnerable position, the rest of the drow rushed Gol'thaga. She kicked the drow leader in the chest to shove her away and pivot. The maul smashed the ribs of the first one, making a full swing over her head to strike the next. Gol'thaga managed to get one more solid hit in before she was completely surrounded. Despite the lithe quickness of the dark elves, Gol'thaga was fast. Much faster than she looked with how big she was. The reach of her weapon made it difficult to get full momentum with it, but it didn't seem to make her any less deadly. She easily blocked and weaved out of most danger. A few nicks and grazes of weapons did get through, the cuts deeper and cleaner than earlier. More numb tingling from these fresh wounds was concerning. That many poisoned blades would eventually be enough to bring her down if the wounds were deep enough.

Gol'thaga bulled the three in front of her into the wall, breaking away from the main mass as much as possible. She raked her claws across their throats while they were pinned there before turning a mighty downward swing onto the first that tried to fill the gap. From there her instincts took over. Another blast of ice and those immediately in front of her went down. She caught the wrist of one woman trying to strike at her side, then swept the legs from another with a one handed swing to her other side. The drow's screams were cut short as Gol'thaga forced the blade of the other, still clutching the assassin by the wrist, through her chest before shifting her grip and giving an upward swing to the face of the doubled over fighter.

She grunted and snarled as a sharp pain went through her side. From the shadows, yet another had managed to slip behind her and thrust a curved blade between her ribs under the arm when her arm was extended. There was a heavy pulse throughout her body before her heart started to beat erratically. The dragonborn captain could feel the poison pumping through her, already numbing and weakening her grip.

The drow seemed to have expected the blow to be enough, as her eyes seemed to widen in surprise as Gol'thaga lashed out and grabbed her by the throat. The vertebrae in the dark elf's neck cracked and splintered in her claws before she flung her assailant into the crowd before her. She wasn't done yet. There was no way she could let them leave. Her team and the clan members they had rescued were depending on her. Besides, there was no way she was going to give poisoners and backstabbers the satisfaction of claiming her life.

The poison was taking its toll already, slowing her down. It wasn't enough to make her an easy target. If anything, she began to fight harder, putting every ounce of strength she had into each blow. Blood spattered far with each hit, but the drow were getting better ones back on her as well. A gash in her arm, a crossbow bolt to her shoulder, a scimitar slash over her thigh, each laced with poison, each making her heart tremor out of rhythm a little more. Breathing heavily, her legs finally gave out and she was forced to prop herself up with her maul to keep from sinking to her knees.

The drow backed away and parted, making a path for the priestess. Her triumphant smirk leered at the powerful dragonborn as Gol'thaga struggled to breathe. "I guess you weren't enough."

Gol'thaga's ragged breath still had enough of a snarl behind it to make a few of the drow flinch as she struggled to stand and keep going. Instead, her grip slipped and she slumped to her knees, still clutching the maul. The priestess was visibly relieved and sauntered over to watch the light fade from the dragonborn's eyes. Gol'thaga willed her heart to keep going, growling threats in the back of her mind to herself.

Get back to work. Are you going to just quit when we need to wipe that smug look off of her face? We are Sivak! We die with honor, not on our knees! Get up!

No matter what she tried to tell herself internally, her body wouldn't hold out. She barely heard the drow priestess say something in her own tongue and her vision was fading as the enormous spider she had been riding slowly crawled towards her. Her lungs let out the rest of her breath as her heart slowly shuddered to a stop.

Just as her eyes began to close, she felt her heart pump once, stronger than ever. Then a second. As if aware of the energy of the earth and feeling it draw into her body, Gol'thaga's eyes snapped open. A green glow filled her eyes, much as it had come from her maul. Her whole body began to radiate this energy.

It wasn't time yet. She had family waiting for her. She needed to bring her daughter home. A primal roar built up inside her that she released with a fury she'd never felt before. As if in slow motion, she saw everything around her. The cowering drow as she stood on her feet, the priestess turning to run, and the spider reaching for her with its long legs. Still screaming, she grabbed the two spindly legs coming towards her. Gol'thaga ripped them from the spider's body with ease, causing it to reel back with a screech.

Without hesitation, she jammed the spider's own leg through its head, cutting its cry instantly. The other leg she was holding was speared through the chest of one drow as she whirled around. Still moving at incredible speed, Gol'thaga grabbed her maul once again and drove the leg completely through the drow and into the woman behind her as easily as nailing two boards together. Another lept toward her, only for the dragonborn to snap her jaws around the dark elf's throat, ripping it free with a twist of her head. Stepping forward, she smashed the knee of another drow, causing her to fall flat so that she could get a clear shot directly in the face of the woman with a hand crossbow behind her. It collided with a cheek and passed through like water, Gol'thaga then finished off the wounded one on the ground by stomping down on her neck.

The priestess could see herself getting backed into a corner and lashed back out at Gol'thaga with her saber. The dragonborn easily ducked her head to the side, not breaking eye contact. The drow struck again, thrusting for Gol'thaga's heart. It was batted away effortlessly by the Sivak captain and as the priestess spun underneath a swing she tried again for Gol'thaga's heart with an ornate dagger she had concealed. Gol'thaga put up her hand, taking the blade in her palm and through the back of her hand. She wordlessly pulled the weapon away from the dark elf and brought it to her mouth. Biting down on the hilt and pulling it free from her hand, she deftly dropped it back into the wounded hand before throwing it. The blade buried itself deep into the throat of the last of the priestess' warriors sulking in the shadows toward her.

The priestess made one final attempt at Gol'thaga with her curved blade, but the dragonborn's response was to take a step back while she swung. Having given herself the distance she needed, the maul crushed the drow's hand, sending the sword sliding across the room. She didn't give the dark elf a moment to cry out as she stepped forward again, driving her foot into her stomach. Winded, the priestess dropped to her knees. She looked up in terror, her eyes pleading for mercy. Gol'thaga did not grant such mercy. Raising her weapon over her head one last time, she brought it down into the drow's skull.

The sudden stillness that signified her victory was little cause for celebration. Gol'thaga stood alone, breathing heavily. Wordlessly, she turned toward the mine entrance, toward home. The propelling energy that had allowed her to continue fighting was slowly ebbing away. Her limbs began to get heavy as the glow around her dulled and faded. She made it to the doorway, snapping the silver thread as her clawed feet scraped the stone. The powerful, steady beat of her heart became faint and erratic while her breathing got shallow.

A loud clang went unnoticed as her maul head hit the floor. The scraping sounds against the metal echoed around her as she dragged her weapon behind her until it became too heavy. She looked at the weapon. Her ancestral weapon of thirty generations. It would only slow her down. She couldn't allow that. She had to get home. Her husband was waiting for her so they could pick up their daughter from the kresh.

Gorgon and Granite

The haft clattered to the ground as she let it go, stumbling forward. She had to keep going, but every step became harder than the last. Her legs would barely move, her vision was getting blurry. Only when she slumped to her knees did she realize it was tears in her eyes that were making it hard to see. Gol'thaga knew she wouldn't make it. Not to the Argentum Bastion, not to home, not into her husband's arms. Her heart was barely shuddering at this point, her breathing nothing but a whisper.

The tears began to roll freely down her face as she closed her eyes. Her nieces had been counting on her to return. Rotta'ghan was waiting. And her daughter. She had been so close. So close to not pretending she didn't know which was hers. So close to holding her for the first time. The tears rolled off her snout and splashed onto the cold stone as her heart quietly stopped. As the last of her breath left her chest, she spoke softly before her eyes closed forever.

"Gol'rotta… I'm sorry…"
Granite

Rotta'ghan felt as though the world was going in slow motion. Dressed in his full armor as with all formal events, he heaved a stretcher up and onto his shoulder. Three others were assisting him, marching slowly much like pallbearers. Taking it to the ceremonial chamber the clan had carved into the base of the mountain long ago, he tried his best not to look at the reflective ice that coated the stone in thick sheets. He and the others brought the stretcher to the center of the small room and placed it onto an obsidian table. Turning, the three saluted and bowed before quietly exiting the chamber.

Alone for a moment, Rotta'ghan looked down at the body on the stretcher with sorrow welling up inside him. His wife, Gol'thaga, lay there before him. Her body was covered in cuts and blood, wounds ranging from minor to grievous. There were several that would have ended a normal person's life immediately. That was something to be proud of in the eyes of most of the Sivak Clan. It brought no peace to him though and was made worse by the streaks in the grime and blood on her face. Gol'thaga had died weeping.

He removed her harness and clothing, gently putting them aside before picking up a pristine white cloth. In the innermost part of the chamber was a pool where a spring came up. Rotta'ghan knelt and dipped the cloth into the ice cold water. Wringing it out, he stood again and held back the pain in his heart as he began to clean the blood from his wife. He washed away all the signs of battle, grabbing a new cloth each time the current was saturated red.

The last part Rotta'ghan washed was her face. He had been unable to bring himself to look at her during the process. Holding her hand in his, he carefully dabbed and wiped away the streaked tears until Gol'thaga was clean, the only evidence she was no longer among the living being the wounds in her now glistening scales. Rotta'ghan squeezed her hand, pressing his forehead to hers. With one last caress of her cheek, he cleared his throat to stop himself from sobbing before sitting down with her attire.

Once he had cleaned the blood out of any of the fabric, the leather needed to be oiled and buttons and buckles needed to be polished. Her weapon lay beside her, waiting to be cleaned as well, the metal hidden as though painted on rather than bloodstained. He had to pause as he got to the last piece. The Tlhogh Stone, the gem he had given her to propose, needed care as well. Rotta'ghan stared at it for a long moment before finally polishing the surface until it sparkled again.

The task done, he redressed Gol'thaga and folded her arms in a position of rest. She deserved to be at peace, so he had placed her in the way she slept, rather than with her arms crossed in front of her chest. Still fighting the lump in his throat, Rotta'ghan took the maul and walked outside the chamber where several clan leaders had gathered, as well as his niece and daughter. Wordlessly, he held out the maul in his palms, bowing to the archivist as he took it from him. Holding out his hands, the two children hurried to him. His niece's little hand held two of his fingers as best they could, but his daughter went to his side, letting his arm wrap around her in a comforting embrace.

Neither had gotten to meet her, but he could see the pain they shared with him. Little B'lanna tried to give him a reassuring smile through the tears welled up in her eyes. His daughter though. Gol'rotta stared forward as if in a state of shock. Rotta'ghan held her a little tighter, getting her to look up for a brief moment.

The three of them walked back into the chamber, followed by the praetor, praetora, Gol'thaga's commanding officer and the kresh mother. Stepping inside, B'lanna gasped and averted her eyes as the obsidian altar came into view. Gol'rotta's eyes stayed fixed on her mother, a hollow gaze with disbelief etched onto her face. The praetor started speaking, something ceremonious that Rotta'ghan barely heard as he started at Gol'thaga much in the same way his daughter was.

"We honor you, Sivak Captain Gol'thaga. A life dedicated to service, a life given in service. Your name shall be remembered as an inspiration, a hero of our clan. Rest now, in your well earned peace and know that the tragedy of your loss shall not be in vain."

The praetor finished speaking, sprinkling a mix of powdered silver and cold iron over

Gorgon and Granite

Gol'thaga's body. With a nod to her family, Rotta'ghan and the two children stepped forward. They all breathed out their dragon's breath, carefully coating her in a layer of ice. The pristine, crystalline case it formed around her was beautiful in its own way, sparkling with the rest of the ice in the chamber around them and protecting her body from the outside world.

With that, Rotta'ghan lined up with the stretcher again, the clan leaders each taking the remaining pall and lifted Gol'thaga. They walked at a slow pace, much of the clan standing on either side of a path leading to the place she was to be buried. Gol'rotta and B'lanna stayed at Rotta'ghan's side, clinging onto him as they trudged to the site. The kresh mother followed behind, making sure that as they carried the fallen warrior the clan members wouldn't crowd them after moving past.

The four carrying Gol'thaga gently lowered her into a hole that had been dug within the burial grounds. It was close to her brother's and surrounded by her ancestors' resting place. Once placed, the praetor, praetora and general bowed their respect to the family before taking their leave. The kresh mother hugged them each individually before taking her leave as well, politely encouraging the rest of the clan to give them some privacy.

The two children stayed silent, Gol'rotta still staring blankly at her mother, willing it to not be true that she was gone. Gone before they even got to meet. Rotta'ghan couldn't bring himself to reach for the shovel yet to cover his wife. They had made such plans, had so many hopes. It was just him now, left to care for two children that he had only just met.

Finally looking at him for the first time that day, his daughter gazed up at Rotta'ghan, tears streaming down her face. She had been trying so hard to be stoic, or maybe it was sinking in, but now that they were alone the tears began to pour. Rotta'ghan dropped to his knees and held her close, letting himself cry with her. Both silent and still, but with no will to keep their tears from shedding anymore. A moment together and they opened their arms to pull B'lanna in as well. When they had let everything they had out, they turned to the grave, only to see that it had already been filled in by some silent force. From the center of the loamy soil was a small iris flower blooming before their eyes. The faeries were watching over Gol'thaga while she rested as well.

With a heavy sigh and a reassuring smile to the children, Rotta'ghan guided them home, hoping they would all be watched over as they tried to make their way without her.

****

A Tale From the Argentum Bastian

Smoke billowed from his mouth as Rotta'ghan exhaled, the smell of tobacco filling the single room house. Had it only been three years? It felt so much longer as the quiet warrior reminisced about the past. The lit cigar between his claws trailed with more smoke as he looked longingly out the window. He missed her. A few moments in the peace of letting his mind wander to happy days, Rotta'ghan rubbed exhaustion from his eyes with his free hand. He was about to take another drag from the cigar when he heard the excited shrieks of laughter from children.

The voices were easy enough to recognize. Gol'rotta and B'lanna, his daughter and niece. He set the cigar in an ashtray, still burning so that he wouldn't waste any or need to relight it. The children burst through the door, his enormous daughter chasing after her much smaller cousin. Many would have sworn Gol'rotta was nearly done with school with how tall and naturally muscular she was, despite not having started at all yet. Conversely, B'lanna looked much younger, despite being a couple months older than Gol'rotta, since she was below the average height and weight for her age.

Rotta'ghan gave an amused smile as the two of them caught their breath before marching up to him. "What's the rush, girls?"

"It's afternoon!" Gol'rotta exclaimed. "You said we had to play outside until the afternoon and then we could practice, remember?"

Rotta'ghan did remember, but he chose to frown. "Practice what?"

"Dad!" his daughter sighed in exasperation. "You promised you'd teach us how to use weapons before we go to the academy!"

"Did I?" Rotta'ghan adopted a bemused look on his face, trying his best not to smile.

"Yes, you did," Gol'rotta said sternly, looking directly into his eyes.

He couldn't help but break the facade and chuckle. "Well if I promised, then I better show you some things so that I don't get in trouble with the faeries."

The two children gave each other a triumphant look as he stood, picking his cigar back up and tucking the end into a corner of his mouth. As they rushed outside, Rotta'ghan grabbed a bag from the trunk at the end of his bed before following them out. They had both grabbed padded vests to practice in. Gol'rotta was already buckled in and ready to go, while B'lanna struggled with the thick, quilted armor. Too bulky for her, Gol'rotta helped her cousin back out and they looked up at their guardian. He could tell they were afraid he would cancel the lesson if they couldn't protect themselves.

Rotta'ghan sighed and knelt next to his niece. "I was worried about that. Been reading this just in case. We'll get you fighting fit."

He handed her a book that had been tucked into the bag and the two looked at it excitedly. Embossed in silver lettering on the cover was the title, Dual Dueling. B'lanna gasped as she flipped through the pages, finding diagrams and tips throughout, most notably, without armor. Gol'rotta smiled at her cousin with relief and approval, patting her on the back before turning back to her father.

"As for you, young lady, you're starting with this," Rotta'ghan reached back into the bag and pulled a hunting knife free.

Her disappointment was plain to see as she reached out and took it. "But… what about mom's weapon?"

"A good warrior knows how to use any weapon," Rotta'ghan said, unsheathing a second knife from his belt. "We'll start with the basics and work up."

He motioned for her to stand next to him and they began going over proper form. The lessons went on for the next year, his daughter working hard and even sneaking off to practice on her own the entire time. She and her cousin took different lessons from the veteran, but each was growing in skill quickly. Teaching them combat skills from such a young age wasn't uncommon in the clan, but it seemed to be something Rotta'ghan's daughter bonded with him strongly over. His niece preferred to read, but never failed to practice with them or at least be nearby. It made every night difficult for him, knowing how much his wife would have loved every moment with the children.

Without surprise, B'lanna had kept constant track of when her sister would be coming home as well. The small house was already pretty full with his own bed and the bunk bed that the cousins shared taking up the most space within. When the children went to play, he would often go to watch the young one the clan called Pip. Rotta'ghan was trying to estimate how much she would grow so that he could make her a separate bed of her own when she arrived from the Kresh.

It was difficult to tell though. Pip was incredibly small, often mocked by some of the children for being a runt. She was the oldest left in the Kresh, but she was half the height of others that were a couple years younger than her. It didn't help that she would often wander around alone, leaving I'rosha's apprentice Kurzsa to follow her almost exclusively. About five years prior, she had been abducted by the Fey in the forest for two weeks and he suspected it had done something to stunt her growth.

A Tale From the Argentum Bastian

Then again, he could be wrong and she'd end up being a late bloomer.

His thoughts were interrupted by the approach of another figure standing next to him as he leaned on the fence. Rotta'ghan didn't speak, but the slight smile at the corners of his mouth turned down and hardened. Trei'zdek, his commanding officer and one of the generals of the clan watched the Kresh with him for a moment, not looking in his direction.

"Hello, old friend," he said, his tone hopeful.

A low rumble from Rotta'ghan's throat was the only response he got as the larger soldier took a cigar from his belt pouch and lit it.

Knowing there would still be no pleasantries, the general sighed and handed a rolled piece of parchment toward Rotta'ghan. His eyes shifted, but he didn't turn his head. Seeing what it was, the embers at the end of the cigar flared and a haze of expelled smoke started to drift around him. Eyes back forward, he continued to ignore the general since they hadn't yet engaged in formalities.

"Why did you put in for Reprieve?" Trei'zdek asked, pushing the parchment towards him.

"I have three kids to look after, Sir," Rotta'ghan stated flatly.

"Everyone capable of fighting is being recalled," Trei'zdek explained. "Even Whiptail is back on active duty. We need you, now more than ever."

Rotta'ghan growled, but took the parchment. "Orders?"

"I've been limiting your deployment as much as I can. It's just a week watching one of the encampments near Myconid territory. You'll be back in time to pick up your niece," the general nodded.

Rotta'ghan nodded curtly before turning to leave. He remained silent even when the general called after him.

"If I could have done anything different for Gorgon, I would have, Granite."

Rotta'ghan ignored him, marching back to his home. The children were still out playing, so the house was deserted. He could hear the two of them smacking sticks together, probably sparring or playing warrior as they called it.

Gorgon and Granite

Opening the drawer in the single dresser that held his things, he was greeted by the familiar sight of his scaled armor. He removed his belt to suit up, when his eyes locked onto the buckle. It was where he had chosen to set the Tlhogh Stone Gol'thaga had given him. He clenched his fist as he looked at it, the polished amber set into the plain metal face, the stag beetle inside perfectly preserved forever.

He missed her so much. Gol'rotta and B'lanna were good kids, and she had to miss out on them. The constant deployment only made him worry about if they were eating enough, or if they got hurt playing. They wouldn't have to be alone if they had Gol'thaga there too. Rotta'ghan slammed his fist onto the top of the dresser, creating a large crack in the polished wood. She should have still been there. The clan had sent her on a suicide mission. Holding the stone to his chest, he couldn't help but blame himself more than the clan. He should have gone instead. He shouldn't have let her talk him out of being the one to go.

The door burst open with his daughter rushing in and her cousin following close behind. "Dad? Is everything okay?"

"We heard a crash," B'lanna elaborated.

Rotta'ghan sighed with a smile, kneeling down to their level and placing a hand on their shoulders. "It's fine. I'm fine. Everything is… fine."

"Do you have to go again?" Gol'rotta's eyes didn't light up as they normally did. She was usually excited to hear what kind of stories he would come back with. "What about Pip?"

"It's just a week," Rotta'ghan patted her cheek affectionately. "Plenty of time."

The two girls relaxed and breathed a sigh of relief as Rotta'ghan pulled all of their foreheads together. When he went to stand, he paused as Gol'rotta stared at the belt buckle draped over his arm. He smiled at her and handed the belt to her, letting her hold and touch the stone. She didn't show it, but she had always felt cheated out of a mother and her silent sorrow was enough for Rotta'ghan to resent the military leaders over the last four years.

Regardless, he wasn't about to disobey his orders and went about suiting up. Buckling the scale mail armor on, Rotta'ghan took his time as best as he could. The first time he ever felt reluctant to go on assignment was after bringing the kids home and it had only grown over the years until it became a lead weight in his stomach every time. It only got worse when his daughter reluctantly handed the belt back to him. He smiled at her and clasped it back on, sheathing his hunting knife.

A Tale From the Argentum Bastian

Gol'rotta hurried to that cabinet where weapons were stored. Still staggering a little at the weight, she proudly brought her father his double headed greataxe. He tested the edge before kneeling down to hug the two children.

"Don't burn the place down while I'm gone," he teased them. "We'll pick Pip up as a family when I get back."

He marched out with his battalion, giving his lieutenants a nod and leaving them to bark out the orders. They moved swiftly, making their path through the Underdark to the assigned outpost. Rotta'ghan had trouble focusing just as he had for several assignments. Even at their pace, he felt the time drag on. He spent much of his time at the encampment staring across the chasm before him, waiting for the week to be over.

It was an uneventful assignment to get. The Myconids on the other side of the underground canyon were neutral. Their mushroom-like appearance and fungal bodies made them strange to be around, but they were peaceful and had always been kind to the Sivak. Lighting a cigar, Rotta'ghan took a long drag before sighing out a thick cloud of smoke. Watching them go about their business was about the only distraction he had from his longing to return home. He mused on that thought quite a while and wondered if there was some irony in it. He was a career soldier. For most of his life he couldn't wait to get his next assignment, but now? Now he could think of a thousand things he'd rather be doing, each involving the children at home.

The smoke from the embers at the of his cigar kept trailing as he stared forlorn across the canyon. He was aware of the sideways glances he had been getting. Whatever they were for, he didn't really care. He and his battalion had done this song and dance so many times that his presence felt like nothing more than a formality at this point. They did their duties without needing orders constantly barked at them and that was all that really mattered.

None of these thoughts made him unattentive though. On the sixth day he blinked, stopping his gaze into the past that could have been and the future he hoped would be. He signaled one of his lieutenants over. Gesturing with a hand, the two listened carefully. The lieutenant was about to speak up after a few moments, but Rotta'ghan cut him off by raising his hand a few inches higher. Faintly, in the distance, the experienced captain could hear it. The rhythmic rumble of an army marching in step. A big one. The duergar were on the move. They were the only ones that weren't concerned about making noise of the denizens of the Underdark. The lieutenant's eyes widened as he eventually picked up the noise as well. Rotta'ghan nodded to him as he stood rigid and alert. It was time to be a soldier.

Gorgon and Granite

"Man the wall!" his lieutenant shouted across the small encampment. "Casters to the towers! Bows at the ready!"

Rotta'ghan took a long drag to finish his current cigar, holding the smoke in before exhaling, heading into the chest in his tent. Taking out a key, he unlocked it just as several of his soldiers entered after him. Passing each of them a case of scrolls, they saluted in turn before going to the elevated platforms used to overlook the canyon and its surroundings. The captain strode with an alarming, gliding grace as he worked through the quickly assembling ranks. Standing at the center of the wall that divided their camp from the beginnings of enemy territory, he nodded to his lieutenant again as the clear sound of metal boots stomped in unison came closer.

"Nock and draw! Wait for your command!"

As one, the archers lining the wall took arrows from their quivers, nocking and aiming down the path in one fluid motion. Not even a minute later, the duergar army marched around the corner. Ranks of them kept coming and though no one showed it, Rotta'ghan could feel the tension in his ranks growing. They were at least five hundred strong, outnumbering the dragonborn nearly ten to one. With cave walls on one side and the chasm on the other, they did have the advantage of holding the choke point, but that was a lot to hope for a victory.

They stopped, one with more intricate armor marching forward and crossing the space until they were equal distance from their army and the wall the dragonborn were guarding. "I come to speak with ye' leader."

Rotta'ghan caught his two lieutenants glancing at him for reassurance. The captain looked the dark dwarf directly in the eyes. "Speak."

"Yer outnumbered. Surrender and le' us pass," the duergar demanded. "Ye'll be treated well iffin ye' cooperate. Resist and die."

Rotta'ghan nearly grinned with pride. Around him he could see jaws set in anger and the creak of bowstrings as they were pulled even further. Such an ultimatum was a good way to guarantee his soldiers had no room for fear. He let out a single exhale, making a snort of laughter before taking out a fresh cigar. He lit in front of the duergar without a single word as he took a few puffs to ensure it burned.

"Did ye' nay hear me, reptile?" the duergar spat.

Rotta'ghan gripped the wall with one hand, jumping over the side. Tucking the cigar into a corner of his mouth, he strode towards the dwarves alone. The duergar that had been speaking smiled with a look of smug superiority as the big dragonborn approached. It melted away into confusion as Rotta'ghan drew his greataxe in a smooth motion off of his back before stopping several paces away. Pointing the head of the axe at the leader in front of him, it was clear to all that could see. The dragonborn was issuing a challenge.

"So be it," the dark dwarf snarled, drawing a heavy mace and his shield.

Still several paces away, the two stood in a fighting stance, facing each other. Rotta'ghan nodded to the dwarf to indicate he was ready whenever he was. The dwarf didn't nod back. He stood there for a few seconds before he went to take a step forward.

Faster than he, or any of the army behind him could blink, Rotta'ghan was already behind him, his axe extended at the end on a full swing. It took a second more, but the dwarf finally moved, only to fall forward as his head rolled off his shoulders. The dragonborn breathed in a long breath through his cigar, pulling it out of his mouth to exhale a cloud of smoke over his head. He tucked it back into the corner of his mouth and pointed at the next duergar wearing an officer's insignia with the head of his axe.

"Jus' kill 'im!" he shouted, a mixture of anger and fear in his shrill command.

As if the wrong side heard the command, as soon as the duergar had shouted, a volley of arrows pierced into the front rank of the army. Before they could react, spells began streaking through the tunnel. Explosions of ice and booming sonic blasts scattering the middle ranks with ease. Several stalactites fell from the rumbling echo and crushed several more. Temporarily deafened and disoriented, the duergar had already taken heavy casualties before they even had the chance to strike.

Rotta'ghan stood casually waiting for the rocks to stop falling, hearing the cries of several through the dust as they were pushed into the chasm. Without waiting for the air to settle, he strode into the cloud of debris. Any glimpse he caught of a duergar soldier and he was there, severing neck or limb with precision cutting. Despite how heavy the weapon was, he was looking to end any fight as quickly as possible. His powerful muscles flexed as he cleaved silently through enemies with ease.

The clanking of metal being bashed together caught his attention as he shoved a dwarven officer into the chasm with a kick. Silently stepping back he could see through the haze enough to see the tortoise formation of shields quickly coming together and advancing. Slipping through the last of the dust, Rotta'ghan made it back to the wall where one of his lieutenants leaned over to offer a hand for him to jump up and grab.

Rather than taking it, Rotta'ghan sprang up with a jump, making it over the top and onto the platform with the archers again.

With a shrug, his lieutenant straightened back up. "Something wrong, captain?"

"Shield cover. Prepare reflex shots and Sleet Storm," Rotta'ghan commanded, ignoring the concerned look his lieutenant was giving him.

The other dragonborn repeated the orders for the rest to hear, with the archers drawing again and the casters preparing to cover the tunnel between them and the enemy in ice. The ammunition would run out eventually and the mages were expending their energy very quickly. There was a very good chance that even if the tides stayed in their favor, it wouldn't last forever.

"Ladybug! Dust-Devil!"

Two of the younger soldiers in the army hurried through the ranks, giving each other confused looks before standing before their captain and saluting. "Yes, sir?"

Rotta'ghan looked at them. Two young girls that had been recently assigned to his unit. They were good soldiers. Smart and brave, skilled enough to make the cut to be in the battalion despite being the youngest of them. "Go get reinforcements. We're counting on you."

The two looked at each other in disbelief before one of them stepped forward. "Sir, we are here to fight. We're not-"

"Obey your orders, soldier," Rotta'ghan snapped.

The girl that had stepped forward went to speak again, but her companion with black speckles in her scales put a hand on her shoulder. Looking to Rotta'ghan, she saluted again. "With all speed, sir."

The captain nodded and turned back, looking down the tunnel at the growing tortoise formation as the dark dwarves marched slowly towards them. Signaling to the mages, they made a few incantations. Two created a wind, causing it to sleet, freezing the ground and making it slick on the pathway to the wall and making visibility poor. The other two prepared to sling more powerful, explosive spells. With attention drawn back to the advancing duergar, Rotta'ghan glanced back to check on the ones he had sent for reinforcements. They were already specks in his vision as they ran as fast as they could. A sense of relief washed over him, allowing him to focus on the battle in front of him.

Rotta'ghan nodded to his lieutenant again, who ordered the casters holding spells to release them into the shield formation. They impacted, but as they did, a shimmer of energy rippled across the shields at the point of impact before the magic dissipated. As they got closer, he could see that even the hail pelting down was vanishing inches from hitting the surface of the plates of metal. The captain held up a fist to halt his mages before they tired themselves out, leaving just the ones maintaining the indoor snowstorm going. Almost immediately after they stopped, the shields shifted and some were pulled back like slats. Crossbows fired in a volley, aimed right at the elevated towers. All four soldiers were wounded, not having a place to go to get out of the way. The dragonborn archers fired back, but the narrow gaps closed again, only to open when they were drawing the next arrow. Another volley cut down two of the casters, incapacitating a third, leaving only the fourth concentrating on the created sleet storm.

About to call for another attempt at breaking the tortoise formation, Rotta'ghan's sharp eye caught a glimpse of a problem. The snow was evaporating around the shields because it was made of magic and glancing down at their feet, the snow and ice was disappearing as the dwarves approached, leaving their footing clear of anything that might slow them down.

"Brace for impact!" he roared.

Spurred into motion, his close combat soldiers rushed the gate of the wall, bracing against it with shield and body while others grabbed beams to line up and reinforce it. As suspected, the shields parted and twenty duergar rushed a battering ram into the door. The entire wall shook and wood cracked, metal screeched as it bent and twisted. The archers managed to find weak points in their armor to kill some of the duergar as they hit, but their bodies were shoved aside and immediately replaced by others before backing up into the tortoise formation again to be walked back for more momentum.

"Bows away! Steel out!" Rotta'ghan bellowed around his cigar. "On my signal!"

The archers immediately strapped their bows over their shoulders and drew various weapons. They waited as the duergar tortoise formation started building up speed again, waiting just until they began to part for the battering ram. As it opened, Rotta'ghan leaped from the wall again, only this time followed by twenty-one of his warriors. Three of them landed directly on the ram, balancing on it as the dwarves were forced to tip into the ground. Rotta'ghan cleaved straight through a dwarven helmet as he landed, slicing all the way until he was halfway down the torso before kicking the corpse away and laying into the shield bearers.

His remaining lieutenant on the wall called for a number of the warriors to come up and replace the archers once the wall was sufficiently braced. Expert marksmanship rained support of the warriors on the ground. Rotta'ghan and the lieutenant that had followed him over bulled into the enemy line, pushing them back. With the opportunity open, a few of the dragonborn that had shields on them clasped their weapon in their teeth before bending down to heft the battering ram into their possession. Four of them managed to lift it without further help and heaved together, throwing it into the canyon before rejoining the fray, not even stopping to take a breather.

The tortoise formation broken and its soldiers falling rapidly, crossbow bolts began streaking across the tunnel again. The next wave of the army was rushing up to meet them. Rotta'ghan grit his teeth as they charged in. They shrugged off or ignored arrow fire, launching themselves at the dragonborn recklessly, without weapons. Battleragers, dwarven warriors that were more like berserker grapplers. They gripped tightly, spiked armor puncturing scales and ripping flesh the more the Sivak soldiers struggled to break free.

Rotta'ghan caught two of them with the head and haft of his axe, shoving them back and winding back with a swift strike that slashed both of their throats . He rushed to his soldiers, burying the edge of his weapon in the skulls of the duergar and pulling them off the dragonborn. Several were already dead. Those that weren't were severely wounded, but they couldn't retreat back through the gate of the wall while the enemy was so close. The soldiers still standing were working their way through the berserkers, but the next wave of duergar were closing in.

Their line ran forward, threatening to engulf the remaining dragonborn on their side of the wall. More crossbows were fired from behind the charging ranks. With their focus divided, the dragonborn archers were caught off guard. Most had been firing down into the berserkers to help their fellow soldiers and were shot from the wall by the heavy dwarven fire. With the heavily armored dwarves filling in the gaps, the dragonborn on the ground were engulfed by their enemy.

Surrounded, the loud banging of metal striking wood caught Rotta'ghan's attention through the din of battle. Many of the duergar had moved past the remaining Sivak warriors and were assaulting the door with their warhammers. Working his way back, the captain ducked and weaved the blows coming from all around him, countering with heavy blows that shredded the thick, dwarven platemail. Despite his efforts, the door splintered and fell.

A Tale From the Argentum Bastian

Rather than the duergar going through though, the dragonborn burst forth, the last twenty still behind the wall pouring out and cutting down their foes as they pushed the line back again. The fresh soldiers had a foracity that easily overpowered the tired duergar. The bodies of dragonborn and dark dwarf were littered across the battlefield, giving both sides difficult footing. Still they both pushed on. Rotta'ghan no longer had the time to assess the fight. They were in a fight for their lives now. The wall was breached, the encampment was useless now despite no one getting past it. Even with all of the skill and experience on their side, they were going to be done in by numbers.

Soldiers around him were falling as each tried to take on three duergar at once. Even with Rotta'ghan moving like a blur across the battlefield to back his men and women up, there just wasn't enough of them. He continued fighting as his muscles ached, watching as the people he'd known for decades, his soldiers, his friends gradually fell round him. People he cared about. People he loved. Yet, with that thought, his mind strayed back to his home where two young girls were waiting for him. Despair was creeping into his thoughts as he began to worry about them. Forcing himself to keep his eyes up, he saw the back of the dwarven line. They were almost through. There were only two ranks left.

Renewed strength had him grip his axe tightly and shove the thoughts away. He swung with brutal efficiency and a steel, cold resolve. Waiting for openings instead of overpowering, going for vitals or removing limbs so that the duergar before his axe were no longer a threat, one way or another. He was going to finish this.

As the next duergar filled the gap, his axe raised again, but as he swung, but as he did the duergar dropped their shield, side stepping and swinging his warhammer with both hands. Rotta'ghan was struck directly in the chest. He could hear his ribs crack and as he was winded and took a forced gasp, the cigar dropped from the corner of his mouth. As he dropped to one knee, the battle went still. As if stunned, both sides parted, stepping back to their respective lines.

Rotta'ghan coughed. He could taste the blood from his lungs filling his mouth. He could live. It was bad, but not over. He had to get home. Staggering to his feet, the dragonborn captain pointed at the duergar that had stuck him. The remains of the army looked to each other in uncertainty before the challenged dwarf stepped forward. The standoff didn't last as long, as the bearded warrior charged. This time Rotta'ghan stepped to the side before grabbing the duergar by the throat. Lifting him clean off the ground and slamming his back into the stone floor, the dragonborn raised his axe above his head before driving it through his adversary. Blood seeped between his teeth as he stood upright again and pointed at the next duergar.

Gorgon and Granite

Instead of waiting, the next challenger rushed in as soon as he was called out by the powerful dragonborn. Rotta'ghan did a low sweep, cutting the dwarf's leg completely off at the knee before swinging again and killing him with a blow to the neck before he even had a chance to fall. As he straightened, he pointed again, wiping a trickle of blood from the corner of his mouth. The next was faster, managing to close the distance enough for Rotta'ghan to have to block and hold him off with the haft of his axe. As they stood locked in place, he slipped one hand to his belt, drawing a knife from its sheath and stabbing it through the duergar's throat.

As his enemy slumped, so did he, coughing and spraying blood across the stone. Sheathing the knife again and wheezing, Rotta'ghan gripped his greataxe on the ground and pointed with a finger this time. As he sputtered and tried to rise again, a hand touched his shoulder. His lieutenant was there, face bloody, main sword arm missing. With a broken smile, he helped his captain up, pointing and issuing a challenge of his own. Following his example, the remaining half dozen of the Sivak soldiers stepped up.

Each of them were battered and bleeding heavily. Some were not going to be able to walk home, some were, but they all challenged the dwarves. Whether out of pity or respect, the duergar answered every challenge. One by one, the few on each side fell in their duels until finally it was only Rotta'ghan and one dark dwarf left. Mustering everything he had to offer, the dragonborn nodded his ready to his last opponent. The dwarf ran at him. Before this distance was closed, Rotta'ghan let the greataxe slip to the very end of the haft and raised it over his head. Swinging a complete circle over his head and the full reach of the greataxe gave full momentum. With a roar, the weapon went through the duergar's neck as if nothing was there.

His enemy fallen, Rotta'ghan dropped to his knees again. Every muscle in his body was on fire, he was winded and breathing heavily from what he was sure was a collapsed lung. In his head, he told himself that he could walk home. He just needed to catch his breath. And then, through his labored breath, he heard the clank of metal boots on stone. Another regiment of duergar was marching on him. He couldn't help but feel his heart sink as he watched them come up a rise in the tunnel, parting to let someone come through.

Coming from the ranks of the duergar, a singular figure stepped forward. Rotta'ghan could see a regal respect to the way he moved and as he came alone to the dragonborn he could see an iron crown on his head. With a sigh, Rotta'ghan fumbled through one of his belt pouches, using the moment as an excuse to look at the belt buckle. There was nothing left he could do.

A Tale From the Argentum Bastian

As much as he wanted to see his girls back home, as much as he had wanted to pick up the youngest from the kresh, it was over.

The duergar king approached as Rotta'ghan put another, fresh cigar in his mouth. The dragonborn fumbled with the lighter, his hand still strained from the battle and growing weak. Kneeling before him, the duergar struck a match and held it out to Rotta'ghan. His eyes showed surprise, but gratitude as he leaned forward to light the cigar. Satisfied the cigar was appropriately lit, the dark dwarf moved the match to a pipe and lit it.

A moment of respectful silence lingered between them as the king surveyed the area. Hundreds of his warriors lay dead, the wall still stood, but needed a new door, and knowing that the Sivak never retreated, the lack of dragonborn bodies was purely because they did not have the numbers to make as many.

"I've heard o' ye'," the duergar said finally. "Yer the one they call Granite."

Rotta'ghan acknowledged with a shift of the cigar.

"Tell me, Granite, are ye' afraid to die?" the king asked.

Rotta'ghan grunted in a way that could only be interpreted as a laugh.

"I thought not," the duergar nodded in approval. "Ye' can't get blood from a stone."

He stood, still barely taller than the dragonborn on his knees and drew a dagger. Rotta'ghan eyed it, but seeing the look on the duergar king's face, he knew the dwarf did not have any pleasure in what he was about to do. The dragonborn nodded and received a nod in return. Embracing Rotta'ghan with one arm, the other pierced the dragonborn's heart with the dagger. His body started to relax as the dwarf respectfully laid him down and placed the greataxe in Rotta'ghan's grip. As he walked away, he signaled to his army, commanding them to turn around and return home.

With the last of his strength, Rotta'ghan reached to his belt to thumb the gemstone at the buckle. With his last breath, Granite, the silent warrior, spoke, willing the words to reach his daughter.

"Sorry, Gol'rotta…but I'm going to be… with your mother again."

* *

CAPTAIN
GOL'ROTTA
It's fine.
I'm fine.
EVERYTHING IS
FINE!